J-SERIES HANK #67 ERICKSON
2016
Erickson, John R.,
Wagons west /

The Wild West

The wagon and I had gotten high-centered in the brush, is the point. I was gasping for air. Alfred's mouth hung open and his eyes were wide with...I don't know, surprise, fear, or excitement, I suppose. I had given him a pretty wild ride.

I needed help but saw no sign of Kitty. "Hey Pete, front and center!" He took his sweet time, of course. Cats always do that and it drives me nuts, but I must admit that I was kind of glad when he came slithering through a crack in the brush. "There you are. Good. Listen, pal, we have a little problem."

He swept his gaze over the scene. "Not a little problem, Hankie."

"Okay, a big problem. How are you at untying knots?"

"Well, Hankie, cats don't do knots." He gazed up at the sky. "And cats don't do *wet* either."

"What does wet have to do with anything?"

He pointed a paw toward the north. "Rain."

I turned my head around and saw...gulp...

Wagons West

John R. Erickson

Illustrations by Gerald L. Holmes

Maverick Books, Inc.

MAVERICK BOOKS, INC.
Published by Maverick Books, Inc.
P.O. Box 549, Perryton, TX 79070
Phone: 806.435.7611
www.hankthecowdog.com

First published in the United States of America by Maverick Books, Inc. 2016.

1 3 5 7 9 10 8 6 4 2

LIBRARY OF CONGRESS CONTROL NUMBER: 2016934001

978-1-59188-167-4 (paperback); 978-1-59188-267-1 (hardcover)

Hank the Cowdog® is a registered trademark of John R. Erickson.

Printed in the United States of America

For Kate, Sam, Todd,
Madeline and Abigail Bahorich

CONTENTS

CHAPTER ONE

A Herd of Sheep

It's me again, Hank the Cowdog. The mystery began on a warm day in the spring. That was the day Little Alfred and I set out in a covered wagon to explore the Wild West and I had to solve the Ominous Riddle of Fog. It was also the day that Pete the Barncat tried to eat a friend of mine.

You probably don't believe that Kitty tried to do such a thing, but he did. We'll get to that in a minute, so be patient.

Spring came hard that year. Which year? Great question. It's important that we get the timing right on these things, because if you start off on the wrong foot, the footer you go, the wronger it gets.

1

We dogs have two right feet, don't you see (the front and the back), but also two wrong feet (the back and the front), so we have to be careful in making these calculations. Timing is crucial in the Security Business.

Even so, I don't remember which year it was. It came after the previous year but right before the next one, and that's as close as we can get. Sometimes we have to use our best estimate. In the Security Business, timing isn't everything.

The important thing is that spring followed winter, but winter didn't want to leave. We had a few pretty days and then got blasted by another cold front—warm day, cold day; pretty day, ugly day with sleet and cold wind, back and forth.

A dog gets tired of that pattern after a while and wishes that winter would just go away and leave us alone, and you'll be surprised to know that we have a Barking Routine that we used to hasten the approach of spring. We called it, "Winter, Take a Hike."

We used it quite a lot that year, but I'm sorry to report that...well, it didn't seem to do much good. It appeared that the weather was doing pretty muchly what it wanted to do, never mind what those of us in the Security Division had to say about it.

I don't suppose you'd want to hear our Barking Routine, would you? You *would*? Well, let's think about that for a second. See, it's pretty heavily classified, which means that we don't allow just anyone to hear it. If the Charlies ever got hold of it, there's no telling how much damage they might cause.

On the other hand, maybe it wouldn't hurt if we lifted the veil just enough to give you a peek. We'll try it and see what happens, but you have to promise not to blab it around. Promise?

Okay, here we go. Check this out.

Winter Take a Hike

Barking Routine #034-66-772

CAUTION!!

Pretty Heavily Classified Information!

Winter, take a hike.
Excuse us, but we'd like
For you to leave, go fly a kite,
Walk or run or ride a bike,
Just go...away!

We're sick of wind and chill.
It's like a dentist's drill.

We've had enough, we've had our fill
Of winter's drab and bitter pill,
So go…away!

We hate to make a scene,
But we must intervene.
We're tired of brown and shriveled things,
So take a hike and bring the green.
And go…AWAY!

End of Pretty Heavily Classified Section
PLEASE DESTROY!

So there you are. What do you think? Pretty awesome, huh? You bet. A lot of people think that ranch dogs just lie around, taking naps and waiting for scraps, but that's only a tiny part of what we do. There are levels to this job that the general public just doesn't know about.

They're not supposed to know. We don't want them to know. We'd much rather conduct our business under the cover of secrecy.

Anyway…where were we? I don't remember.

Does anybody remember what we were discussing?

Huh. I'm drawing a blank.

Wait, hold everything. Springtime. Now we're

cooking.

Okay, as usual, my day started before daylight and I had already barked up the sun by the time Loper and Slim showed up at the machine shed. They climbed into a pickup and drove off to a field east of headquarters. As I recall, they were plowing the ground and planting feed, and seemed to be in a hurry to get it done before a rain.

The weather report on the radio was calling for a 50% chance of thunderstorms, don't you see. Normal people see that as a 50% chance of nothing, but ranchers and cowboys get excited about it.

I gave them an escort all the way to the mailbox, then returned to headquarters and put in a few hours doing Bird Patrol. See, the downside of springtime is that we get an invasion of tweet-tweets. They come from everywhere and perch in my trees, *without permission to perch in my trees,* and we're talking about thousands of little birdie trespassers.

And you talk about NOISE! They tweet. They twitter. They squeak, squawk, whistle, warble, flitter, flutter, flap, and fly. A dog can hardly take a decent nap...that is, it's almost impossible for us to conduct Ranch Business with all the noise.

We have to attend meetings, don't you know,

endless meetings: the Budget Committee, the Long Range Planning Group, the Weather Committee, the Commission on Cats...the list goes on and on. So, yes, after doing Bird Patrol, I was chairing a meeting of the Long Range Planning Group, when a stranger burst into the room and delivered some alarming news.

"Hank, you'd better wake up. A bird just hit the window."

I didn't recognize the guy. He must have been a new employee. I looked up from the sprawl of spreadsheets that covered the conference table, blinked my eyes, and studied his face. It was located on the front of his head and consisted of one nose, one mouth, and two eyes.

That checked out, but I still didn't recognize him. "Calm down. You said a herd bit the window?"

"No, a bird hit the window."

"A herd of what—cattle, buffalo, deer, sheep? Be specific."

"Not a herd. A bird."

"Okay, you heard a bird, so what? Listen, pal, I've been hearing birds every second of every day for the past two weeks. They're driving me nuts, so don't tell me about birds. Furthermore, you've interrupted this meeting."

"What meeting?"

"The meeting that was meeting. You've interrupted a very important..." I took a closer look at his face. "How long have you been working here?"

"Oh...forever, I guess."

"Then you should know better than to burst into the muddle of a meedle."

"I think you were asleep."

"You keep talking about sheep. What are they doing on this ranch?"

"Not sheep. SLEEP."

"Of course sheep sleep, but sheep have no business sleeping on this outfit. This is a cattle ranch and..." I rose from my chair, with the intention of pacing around the room. It's something I do to concentrate the hocus of my pocus, only this time something went awry with my legs. I lurched to the left and collapsed on the floor. "Sorry. My leg must have gone to sleep."

"Yeah, along with everything else."

"I beg your pardon?"

"You've been sleeping all morning."

"How dare you..." I hoisted myself up on all-fours and took a moment to gather my thoughts. "All right, let's get to the bottom of this. Who are you and what are you doing here?"

He heaved a sigh and rolled his eyes around. "I'm Drover."

"Wait, hold it right there. I have a runt on my staff named Drover. Does that strike you as odd?"

"No, 'cause it's me. I'm the real Drover. Hi."

I looked closer at him and...hmm...paced a few steps away. "Drover, you could have saved us a lot of trouble if you had identified yourself, instead of blabbering nonsense about sheep and goats and buffalo."

"You were asleep."

"I was NOT asleep, and I'll thank you to stop spreading lies! Now, for the last time, tell me about the sheep."

"There aren't any sheep. A bird hit the window."

"We don't have any windows."

"Up at the house. It keeps flying into the window glass."

I gave that some thought. "Oh, I see now. Yes, those birds do this every spring, crash into windows. They're such fools."

"It's a little owl. I think you know her."

"I don't know any owls. I don't socialize with owls."

"Remember Madame Moonshine?"

"Never heard of her. Now, if you'll...did you

say Madame Moonshine? A little owl?"

"Yep, that's her."

I stared at the ground for a long moment. "I know her."

"Hee hee. I told you."

"Please don't giggle and gloat when you happen to get something right."

Then Drover moved closer and delivered some shocking news. "If she knocks herself out on the glass, Pete's waiting to eat her."

PETE?

And so the crisis began, with Drover bringing the news that one of our precious little birdie friends was in danger of being devoured by the cat.

Pretty scary, huh? You bet.

CHAPTER TWO

Rocket Dog to the Rescue

Drover's words caused my head to snap to attention. "What! Pete is going to…stand by, soldier, we're fixing to Launch All Dogs!"

Have we discussed my Position on Birds? Maybe not, but maybe we'd better. A lot of your ordinary mutts consider birds a nuisance. Ordinary mutts bark at the birds and try to chase them away.

Me? I've always taken a more enlightened position. Yes, birds cause a certain amount of distraction, but THINK OF ALL THE BEAUTY THEY BESTOW UPON OUR RANCH.

The flinches and the robinsons and the oreganos add color to a drab world. The song of the markingbird breaks the monotony of long days, and the little swillers are so graceful as they swoop and turn in the air—feathered poetry, you might say. What kind of dreary world would this be without our birds?

But don't expect your ordinary run of mutts to notice any of that, and most of all, don't expect any kind of Art Appreciation from a scheming, selfish little ranch cat. Do you suppose that cats give a rip about feathered poetry or lovely bird songs? They don't. You know what cats do with our precious little birdie friends?

EAT THEM.

That was the crisis facing us. Our local cat was lurking and scheming and waiting for an opportunity to cheap-shot one of the feathered visitors on my ranch, and I was just the dog to bring it to a screeching halt.

I dived into my Rocket Dog suit, turned the dials to the Blast-Off Position, and went roaring away from the Security Division's Vast Office Complex. Oh, you should have seen it! I went swooping over trees and buildings, and executed a smooth landing on the gravel drive behind the ranch house. There, I shucked off the RD suit and rushed to the yard gate.

It took me several moments to reconoodle the situation and gather up the pieces of the peesle.

The puzzle, that is, the puds of the piddle. The piccoo of the petal. Phooey.

It took me several moments to peddle the puddle...it took me several moments to peedle together the piddles of the...let's just skip this.

It really burns me up when this happens. I mean, a guy gets all excited about describing an important event, but when the words come out of his moth, they've turned to mush. Nonsense. Gibberish. It makes him sound...well, not too bright.

Let's slow things down and try this one more time. What I saw was a complicated scene. A bird, a little prairie dog owl, was fluttering its wings, hovering in front of a window on the second story of the house, and jabbering some kind of nonsense. Now and then it crashed into the window. Meanwhile...

The cat was sitting on the sidewalk below—smirking, twitching the end of his tail, and staring up at the activity on the second level. Anyone could see that he was up to no good.

I turned to my assistant, who had just arrived, huffing and puffing. "I know that bird. It's Madame Moonshine."

"Yeah, I told you."

"Stop telling me what you told me."

"Yeah, but I was right, wasn't I?"

"You were lucky."

"What's she doing up there?"

That was a good question. I wasn't sure what she was doing, but it looked pretty strange. It appeared that she was screeching at someone. She said, "Imposter! Usurper! Lowly woodpecker, pretender to the Feathered Realm! Away, away, be gone!"

She delivered that message in a screechy owlish voice, and then...this was really strange... she crashed into the window. For a second, it appeared that the impact would cause her to fall to the ground. In fact, she did lose altitude, but at the last second, she flapped her way out of trouble and swooped back to the window.

And the cat was waiting and watching down below.

Drover said, "I just figured it out. She sees her reflection in the glass and thinks it's another bird."

"That's absurd."

"Gosh, that rhymes."

"You're wasting time."

"That rhymes too."

"Get to the point, if you have one."

"She sees herself in the glass. You did that

once. Remember that time with the mirror? You saw yourself in the mirror and thought it was a Phantom Dog. Hee hee. Boy, that was funny."

I gave him a scalding glare. "Drover, I don't know what you hope to gain by spreading lies about your commanding officer, but let me warn you. This conversation could end up in your permanent peppermint."

"My what?"

"Your permanent record."

"You don't remember barking at the mirror?"

"Of course I don't remember. I don't remember a lot of things that never happened."

"Yeah, but it happened, honest."

I rewound the Tape of My Life and turned my mind back to that afternoon in the machine shed, and remembered...well, I was barking at my reflection in a stupid mirror. "Okay, maybe I remember, but there's a huge difference between what I did and what that bird is doing."

"No, it's the same thing."

"It is NOT the same. She's a bird and I'm a dog. I will always be a dog. I'm proud to be a dog, so stop trying to say that I'm a bird." He shook his head and crossed his eyes. "And stop crossing your eyes when I talk to you."

"Talking to you is hopeless."

"Well, hopeless is better than no hope at all. The point is that I am not a bird."

"I never said you're a bird."

You see what I have to live with? Endless arguments about nothing. Drover gets a crazy idea in his head and...oh well.

I paced several steps away and gazed up at the sky. "All right, listen up. I've reviewed all the evidence in this case and here's the situation. That owl sees her reflection in the window glass and thinks it's another bird. She's attacking the image in the glass. In small but tiny ways, it reminds me of my encounter with the Phantom in the Mirror."

"I'll be derned. I never would have thought of that."

"Yes, well, you have no mental discipline. You just spout whatever nonsense comes into your head."

"Sorry. I'll try harder next time."

"Good. Now, let's put this episode behind us." I paced back to him and laid a paw on his shoulder. "Are you sorry you said I was a bird?"

"Oh yes, and I'll never say it again. What about the cat?"

"The cat is not a bird either."

"Yeah, but he's fixing to eat one. Look!"

Huh? I turned my gaze back to the house, just in time to see a tragedy unfoiling before my very eyes. The owl crashed into the window so hard, it knocked her senseless, and she fell like a rock into the flower bed. An instant later, the cat sprang off the porch and landed on top of the bird.

Drover let out a gasp. "Oh my gosh, what'll we do?"

My mind was racing. "We have no choice. We must send troops over the fence. We have to save Madame Moonshine from the cat."

"I agree."

"Okay, here's the plan. You go in the first wave, just in case Sally May comes out with her broom. Lay down some heavy barking."

His eyes blanked out. "Her broom?"

"Right, it's no big deal. Get in there and kick out some big barks."

"Help!"

"You can do it, son. Remember: this is for the birds!"

He gave that some thought. "You're right. Here I go!" He pointed himself toward the yard fence and went charging off like...

Oh brother. You'll never guess what happened next.

The Dreaded Broom

Maybe you guessed what Drover did, because it was entirely predictable, entirely in keeping with his miserable record with the Security Division. But somehow it caught me by surprise.

After convincing his commanding officer that he was ready to dive over the fence and rush into combat, he dashed two steps forward, swerved left, cut a half-circle on the gravel drive, and went sprinting straight toward the machine shed.

"Hey Drover, you're heading the wrong way!"

"This is for the birds, bye!"

Huh?

Do you see what he was doing? He was quoting me against myself, the very lowest form of treachery.

I should have known that he would take the weenie's way out, but I had dared to hope, dared to believe that this time might be different. It wasn't. He scampered up the hill, dived through the slot between the big sliding doors, and vanished inside, leaving me stunned and crushed with disappointment.

"Drover, come out of there and report to the front! Drover! I'm ordering you to…you will be court-martialed for this!"

For a moment of heart beats, I thought about marching up the hill and jerking him out of the machine shed by his ear, but that would have taken time, and time was something we didn't have.

Don't forget the tragic scene that was taking shape inside the yard. A friend of mine was about to be devoured by the local cat. I whirled around and rushed to the yard gate, and here's what I saw.

Poor Madame Moonshine had knocked herself unconscious on the window glass and lay potsrate in the flower bed. Pete stood over her, licking his chops and beaming an evil smile. I had to do something, and fast.

"Okay, Pete, paws in the air! Back away from the victim, and don't try anything foolish. Move!"

His cunning eyes slid around and landed on me. "My, my, the cops are here."

"You got that right, Kitty. Back away, move it!"

"Now Hankie, we needn't make a scene. It's only a bird."

"That's no big deal unless you're the bird."

"But Hankie, you don't even like birds. You've spent half your life barking at them."

"This is different, Kitty. Not only is that bird a friend of mine, but you're not. Leave the bird alone."

He fluttered his eyelids. "And if I don't, you'll...do what? Jump the fence and come into the yard? Sally May's inside the house and so is her broom. She doesn't allow dogs in her yard, remember?"

"Pete, you're despicable."

"You keep saying that, Hankie, so..." He snickered. "...maybe it's true." He turned his gaze back to the bird. His eyes crackled with sheer delight and he ran his tongue across his lips. "Well, you run along, Hankie. Maybe we can talk...after lunch."

"Don't do this, Pete, I'm warning you."

He ignored me, of course, and I had to stand there and watch. Have you ever seen a cat that has just captured a bird? They go through the same silly routine, every time.

He picked up the bird in his mouth, turned his back on me, pinned down his ears, flicked the last two inches of his tail back and forth, and...this was the part that really got my goatee...he unleashed an eerie sound from somewhere deep in his cheating little throat.

It started in the high range of yowling, a cheap imitation of a police siren, and worked its way down to the low range, a cheap imitation of growling. Obviously he was yowling and growling at ME, since I was the only one around, and maybe he thought...what? That it would scare me so badly, I would run away and hide under my bed?

Ha. You know, cats have a primitive form of intelligence, about the level of a tapeworm. They're experts at lying, cheating, stealing, and spreading chaos, but they don't understand dogs at all. Hey, if you want to get a dog pumped up and ready for war, all you have to do is find some misguided little ranch cat to yowl and growl.

That'll do it. Every time. I mean, it comes like a surge of electricity. It's as though we're hearing a hundred-piece band, playing a stirring march by John Phillip Salsa.

Ten thousand kilowhoops of electricity shot down my backbone. My ears leaped up and in my deepest heart, I sensed that I was about to surrender myself to the savage delight of being a dog—a dog on a righteous mission.

I hit engines one and two, and went flying over the...actually, I aimed a little low on the first try and rammed the fence. No big deal. In moments of high passion, we often get faulty readings on our instruments and misjudge...but the imported poink is that on the second attempt, I cleared that fence like a deer, hit the ground, and came up loaded for bear.

The cat was shocked. I rolled the muscles in my enormous soldiers and took a step forward. "Drop the bird."

Any creature with half a brain would have dropped the bird and run for his life, screaming and terrified, but not old Pete. Oh no. Instead, he held onto the bird, turned up the volume of his yowling, and began edging backward, totally unaware that this was the equivalent of tossing gasoline into a roaring fire.

Then, in a flash, he turned and ran, still yowling and still carrying the bird in his cheating, scheming little mouth. He hopped through the iris patch and dashed around the northwest corner of the house.

Foolish cat. I hit Sirens and Lights, and went

into a full-scale Code Three Pursuit, and we're talking about...

"Hank!"

...Massive Barks and plowing everything that got in the way. Oh, you should have...

"Leave the cat alone!"

...been there to see it! Kitty had played with fire and gasoline, and now he had an explosion heading right for his tail section. Boy, you talk about fun and excitement! Dogs are born for moments like this.

I tracked him on radar and caught up with him in the front yard. There, I locked him into the computer and armed the weapon. I was about to blast him into next week, when he dropped the bird and clawed his way up the trunk of a chinaberry tree.

I bent down, lifted the poor wounded owl into the tender embrace of my jaws, beamed a victorious look at the treed cat, and yelled, "Muff wuff wuff muff muff wuff!" See, I had a mouthful of bird, but I was saying, "Let that be a lesson to you, Kitty. Never mess with a friend of the Security Division!"

I was a little surprised by his response, I mean, he was still wearing his insolent smirk, and somehow that didn't fit. Then he said,

"Hankie, look behind you."

Huh? Look behind me? I seldom do anything a cat tells me to do, but this time I had a feeling...I turned my head and looked around and saw...

Gulp.

Sally May. And her son, Little Alfred.

Where had they...perhaps my Code Three Barking had...

Uh oh.

Well, this looked bad. Not only had I entered her yard and treed her scheming little cat, but I was holding...well, a semi-conscious bird in my jaws, so they might very well have thought...oh brother.

Alfred's expression revealed shock and surprise. Sally May's expression was a lot worse than that. She looked...upset, shall we say, even angry, and she had her hands parked on her hips, always a bad sign.

She glared down at me. "Are you eating birds? Don't we give you dog food?"

What? Eating birds? Hey, I was SAVING birds, but...yipes, when a dog gets caught...

I, uh, lowered my head and, in the tenderest and gentlest way possible, deposited the wounded owl upon the grass at the feet of Our Beloved Ranch Wife. Then I looked up at her and, with eyes and tail wags, delivered a message from my heart.

"Sally May, I know this looks bad. In fact, it looks very bad, and I know that our relationship has had its ups and downs, but hear me out. I think I can explain everything, no kidding. See, your little sneak of a cat..."

She wasn't listening. She turned to her son. "Honey, go get my broom."

Huh? Broom?

The boy dashed off to the house, while his mother glared icicles at me and muttered, "Eating birds. Honestly!"

There are times when a dog should stick around and patch up his relationships, and there are times when he should disappear. When the children are sent into the house to fetch the broom, it's time for the dogs to move along.

I was about to make my exit, when Madame Moonshine's eyes popped open. And let me tell you, when an owl pops her eyes open, it's a little creepy. Those were some strange eyes, huge and yellow.

She stared at me for a moment. "My goodness! It's Hank the Rabbit!"

Let me point out that I had never been a rabbit in my whole life, and surely Madame knew that, but for some reason, she had always insisted on calling me Hank the Rabbit. You figure that one out.

"Uh...it's Hank the Cowdog, ma'am. Hi."

"And unless this has all been some kind of outrageous dream, you saved my life! Oh, thank you, Rabbity Hank, 'twill come back to you as a blessing."

The door opened and out stepped Little Alfred with his mother's broom.

I needed to scoot, but I couldn't resist taking one last shot at the cat. I turned and looked up into the tree. "Hey, Pete, I haven't seen such a pout on your face since the last time I ran you up a tree. I guess you're not having such a good day, huh?"

"It's about to get better, Hankie."

"Oh yeah? Not if I can..."

WHOP!

"Stay out of my yard, leave the cat alone, and stop eating birds!"

Huh?

Okay, that was Sally May's voice and also her broom, and perhaps I had stayed too long.

WHOP!

Yes, too long. It was time to leave.

CHAPTER FOUR

Twucks in the Yard

She tagged me twice with the broom, but missed the third shot. Do you know why? Because I hit Full Turbos and scrammed out of there. When the broom came down, I was gone. Oh, and get this. She swung so hard, when the broom hit the ground, the handle broke in half.

As I was soaring over the fence, I heard her screech, "Disobedient hound! Now look what you've done. You broke my broom!"

I broke her broom? Oh brother. You see what I have to put up with around here? What was I supposed to do, sit there like a stump and get flogged in front of her rotten little cat?

You know, it's very discouraging when we get accused of crimes we didn't commit. Number

One, I didn't break her broom. Number Two, I hadn't eaten any birds, and Number Three, she should have known that *dogs don't eat birds*.

Okay, let's be honest. Sometimes dogs eat birds, but not burrowing owls. No dog in his right mind would eat an owl. Owl meat is tough, stringy, and tasteless. If a dog goes to the trouble to eat a bird and sift through two pounds of feathers, he'll choose a nice, plump, juicy....

Wait. Let's think about this. Telling the truth is always the best policy unless it creates the wrong impression. See, I wouldn't want the little children to get the idea that I...well, go around bumping off chickens. Slurp.

Excuse me. Please disregard that slurping sound. I was misquoted.

The point is that Sally May's chickens are a constant source of temptation. I will admit that. But let me hasten to add that the measure of a dog's character lies in his ability to look temptation straight in the eye and say slurp.

Excuse me. The measure of a dog's character lies in his ability to look temptation straight in the eyeballs and say, "NO!"

Don't forget that the Head of Ranch Security gets paid to protect our chickens from the bad guys. We don't get paid *much*, because this is a cheap-John ranch operation, but part of the deal is that we have to control our craving for…

You know, this is taking us in the wrong direction. Let's drop this discussion about you-know-whats and go back to what I said before. Dogs do not eat birds, especially owls, and it almost broke my heart that Our Beloved Ranch Wife had accused me of doing the very thing that her rotten little cat was trying to do—eat a bird!

I try so hard to please her. I want to be the Dog of Her Dreams, but sometimes I wonder if that will ever happen. Oh well. We have to plug on with our lives, sustained by the belief that one of these days, THE CAT WILL PAY.

Once I had escaped from Sally May and her broom, I spent some time hiding in the cedar trees north of the machine shed. There, I set up an observation post and did Surveza of events in the back yard.

Surveillance, I guess it should be. I did Surveillance.

Sally May and Alfred found a little cardboard box and made a bed for Madame Moonshine, where she could recover from her collision with the window glass—and from her near-miss with the cat. Don't forget that part.

Ten minutes later, she was standing on her

own legs, and ten minutes after that, she had recovered enough to fly. She landed on the yard fence and perched there for a while, then spread her wings and flew off to the south. Sally May and the boy were so pleased, they clapped their hands and waved goodbye.

While this was going on, I turned my field glasses on the cat. He had climbed down out of the tree and I zoomed in on his face. That was one unhappy cat and he had SULK written all over his face. Hee hee. I loved it.

Well, this had turned out about as well as it could have. I had saved a poor helpless bird and had ruined the morning for a pampered, selfish, ungrateful little ranch cat—a good morning's work in anyone's book.

I had lost a few points with Sally May, but maybe I could earn them back another time.

I laid low in the cedar trees and allowed time to heal old wounds. It was really boring, sitting there with nothing to do. Ho hum. For a while, I watched a column of red ants, each one struggling to carry a weed seed that was bigger than itself.

They do this every day, you know. It's their job, dragging seeds down little trails they've tramped out in the dust, and hauling them... where? To their den, I suppose, a hole in the ground. And, believe it or not, these ants were singing. No kidding. You want to hear their little "Ant's Song?"

Ant's Song

For our winter feed,
We perform our deeds.
We must haul our seeds,
Through the grass and weeds,

From the first of May,
Back and forth all day,
We receive no pay.
Never get to play.
It's our job.

So we trudge trudge trudge.
Like a drudge drudge drudge.
Never hold a grudge.
Wish we had some fudge.

To the den, to the trail,
A relentless tale.
At the pace of a snail.
Not a whine or wail.
It's our job.

Not a great song, but not bad for a bunch of ants. Actually, we can learn from the ants. One important lesson is that, if a dog gets so bored that he finds himself watching bugs, he should consider how boring life must be for the bugs, lugging seeds around eighteen hours a day.

But it didn't take me long to get my fill of Ant Wisdom, and I began looking around for other forms of entertainment. I chewed on a stick for a while and dug a hole—again, not very exciting, so I turned my attention back to the house.

Whilst Baby Molly sat in her swing seat, Alfred and Sally May played "Twucks" in the

yard. (In Kid Language, "Twuck" means "Truck," don't you see, and we'll talk more about this in our Vocabulary Lesson. Don't miss it). Sally May got down on her hands and knees, and pushed a big yellow truck around in the grass. She was a good sport about it and tried to make the sounds of a big diesel engine, but...well, she came up a little short.

After a while, the boy looked at her and frowned. "Hey Mom, you sound like a lawn mower, not a twuck."

"Alfred, I'm doing my best."

"Do it like this." Pushing his truck, he produced an amazing blast of noise, as well as a spray of water droplets.

Sally May flinched and wiped her cheek. "Sweetie, try not to spit on your mother."

"Mom, that's what twucks do."

She laughed. "All right, I'll give it a try." She puckered her mouth and threw heart and soul into the effort of being a truck, but...I don't know, she just didn't seem to have a talent for it. After a while, she gave up and rose to her feet. "You win the Battle of the Trucks. Now I have to go start the lunch." Her eyes narrowed and she glanced around. "Don't let Hank bother my cat."

"Okay, Mom."

She went into the house and left a yard filled with the sounds of a happy truck at work. I waited for a couple of minutes, just to be sure the coat was toast...toast was close...*the coast was clear*, there we go. I waited to be sure the coast was toast and ventured down to the yard.

The boy was so busy with his trucking business that he didn't notice me coming his way, but Pete noticed. He isn't very smart but he's fairly observant. I mean, this is a cat that has no job, no responsibilities, and no friends, so what else can he do to while away the hours? He lurks in Sally May's flower patch and stares out at the world.

I picked up the flash of his gaze when I got within fifty feet of the fence. It was coming from the iris patch, of course, his favorite loafing spot on the ranch. He had no idea that I was equipped with laser-sensitive equipment and was monitoring his every move.

That was only one item in a long list of things he didn't know about Security Work. We have sensing devices that no cat has never even dreamed of.

So, yes, I was aware of his every move. Actually, his "every move" didn't amount to much. He was just sitting there, too lazy to do anything but stare and purr, and you'll be impressed that I was also perking up his pickering...picking up his purring on Audio Scanners, another very sensitive piece of equipment.

I reached the yard gate, sat down, and waited for Alfred to be thrilled that I had arrived. Minutes passed, filled with the sputter and rumble of his truck, and he still didn't notice, so I turned to the cat.

"You can quit staring at me any time, Kitty."

"Was I staring at you?"

"Of course you were. I've had you on radar for the past twenty minutes."

"Oh really." His head and tail rose from the iris patch. He was wearing his usual insolent smirk. "I'm sorry, Hankie, I didn't mean to stare. I guess I was just...well, curious."

"Yeah? Be curious about someone else." A moment passed. "Curious about what?"

"Oh, you wouldn't be interested."

"Exactly right. I couldn't care less, but it's my job to know what's going on around here, so...out with it."

"Well, Hankie, I was just curious to know..."

"Hurry up."

"I was curious to know if you were wearing any...hee hee...broom tracks."

I felt my lips twitching into a snarl. "Watch your mouth, Pete, you're playing with fire."

"I know, Hankie, but it's so much fun, I can't resist." He came slithering out of the iris patch, carrying his tail straight up in the air like an…I don't know what. He rubbed his way down the fence and came toward me.

He narrowed his eyes and looked me over. "Hmm, yes, several broom tracks. She really whopped you good."

"She whopped me good, but you didn't get to eat the bird."

"I didn't eat the bird, but you got blamed for it."

"I got blamed for it, but you got parked in a tree."

"It was good exercise, Hankie."

"Yeah, and you need it. You could lose a few pounds."

"It's just more of me for Sally May to love."

"How would you like to climb another tree?"

"How would you like some more broom tracks?"

"She broke the broom."

"She has a mop and you'd look darling wearing mop tracks."

"Oh yeah? You'd look darling with a fat lip."

You know, I love the drama of grilling a

witness in a court of law. It seems to bring out all my savage instincts, and on this occasion, I had old Pete against the ropes and was pounding the daylights out of him. One more minute and he would have been a greasy spot on the cutting-room floor of the court house, but just then a truck came by and ran over his tail.

CHAPTER FIVE

The Burrfessional Eggsplorer

"Reeeeer!"

Old Pete jumped two feet in the air and highballed it back to the iris patch. What a victory! "And let that be a lesson, you little fraud! Court is dismissed!"

Wow. I had mopped the floor with him. A little humor there, did you get it? See, we'd been arguing about mops and I had MOPPED the... maybe you got it, but the point is that my cross-examination had blown Kitty Kitty to smithereens.

Hee hee. Boy, it was the funnest thing I'd done in weeks.

Oh, were you wondering how a truck had gotten into a court of law so that it could run over the cat's tail? Great question, and here's the scoop on that.

Little Alfred was playing trucks in the yard, right? Well, Kitty had gotten so absorbed with running his mouth and showing disrespect for our entire judicial system, he'd stopped paying attention to everything else in the world. The boy saw his opportunity and...

What a fine lad! He had a truck, he saw a tail, and he did what any normal, red-blooded, patriotic American boy would have done. He ran over the cat's tail and sent him back to the bushes where he belonged.

But suddenly a mysterious voice came out of nowhere. "Alfred, don't be mean to the cat!"

Oops. It was the voice of Radar Woman—She Who Saw Everything. She'd been working at the kitchen sink and looking out the window.

Alfred flinched. "Okay, Mom." He turned to me and whispered, "I got caught."

Right. I knew all about getting caught. On this outfit, dogs and little boys can hardly scratch a flea or swat a fly without getting into some kind of trouble. I would be the last dog in the world to say a critical word about the Lady of the House, but...

Good grief, does she have to notice EVERYTHING? I mean, would the world fall apart if she missed one naughty deed?

Oh well. She's a fine lady…a little strange sometimes, but a fine lady.

Alfred looked at me through the hog wire fence. "Hankie, you want to come into the yard and play twucks?"

Well, as far as I was concerned, that was a great idea, but his mother had rules about Dogs In the Yard. I had already tripped her alarm once that day and didn't need to push my luck. Better not, thanks.

He lapsed into a thoughtful moment. "Hankie, you know what I want to be when I grow up?"

I gave that some thought. A truck?

"I'm going to be a burrfessional eggsplorer, like Daniel Boom."

I cocked my head to the side. A what? A "burfessional eggsplorer?" Hmm. That was a new one on me.

You know, I'm pretty good at translating Kid Language into Bow Wow, but every once in a while, he pitches one past me. When that happens, we have to pull up our Language Analysis Program and give it some serious study.

Have we discussed the LAP? Maybe not. It's a great tool and it helps us bridge the language barrier between dogs and children. Do we have time for a demonstration? Sure, let's crank it up and see what we can learn.

Okay, we'll start by looking at the individual words. "Burrfessional" is kind of a long word, but we can break it down into parts: *burr-fession-al*. A bur is a wild plant with stickers. We have several varieties on this ranch: sandburs, cockleburs, and goat-head sticker weeds.

"Fession" is harder to figure out, because... well, it doesn't seem to mean anything, so we have to guess what it might mean if it meant something. "Fession" sounds almost the same as "fashion," so let's go with that.

When we put the two words back together, we have "bur fashion," in other words, somebody wearing clothes made out of sandburs, cockleburs, or goat-head stickers. That sounds odd, doesn't it, so let's hurry on to the next part and maybe things will improve.

If you spend too much time thinking about this stuff, you'll never make it to the finish line.

"Eggsplorer." Yes, this is better, because right away, we see that the first half of the word is something we dogs crave and adore: EGGS. At morning Scrap Time, we'll take an egg any way it's offered: fried, scrambled, hard boiled, soft boiled, hard yoke, soft yoke, no yoke, yoke-broke, under-easy, over-easy, or over-cooked.

Actually, one of our very favorite menu items is the poached egg, and I must tell you that in my line of work, "poached" has a hidden meaning. Heh heh. See, we're not talking about eggs cooked in a pan of water. We "poach" our eggs in the chicken house, don't you see, pluck 'em right off the vine, so to speak, and...hmm, that's probably all we'd better say about this.

In fact, let's erase that part about poached eggs. We said nothing about poaching eggs. Thanks. You might not understand what it means, but your parents will...and so would Sally May if she happened to be listening.

Okay, let's move on to the next part of the so-forth: Daniel Boom. This will be easy as pie. "Daniel" was a famous lion tamer and "boom" is a sound that growing boys love to make, and now we're ready for the big moment when we put everything back together and get the whole translation.

Are you ready? Here we go.

TA-DAH!

When Little Alfred grows up, he wants to be a lion tamer in a circus, who makes a lot of noise, eats eggs all day, and wears a suit of clothes made of sticker weeds.

Is that amazing or what? You never would

have guessed…wait, hold everything. Let's back up and take another look at this.

"Burrfessional eggsplorer like Daniel Boom." You know, in certain respects, it could be translated as "professional explorer, like Daniel Boom." Do you suppose…

Phooey.

You know, the problem with all this high-tech equipment is that sometimes it backfires and we get garbage, and we're talking about total garbage, not partial garbage. The Language Analysis Program is great when it works, but when it goes on the fritz…

Look, one of the problems in being smarter than ordinary dogs is that you sometimes outsmart yourself. We should keep things simple. Simple is always best. Try to remember that.

Where were we? I have no idea. I've exhausted myself on nonsense and…

Wait! Here we go. Alfred had just announced that he wanted to become a famous "eggsplorer," which we've already translated to mean "explorer."

I barked my approval. "Good for you! Sounds like a plan."

He gazed off into the distance. "But if you're going to be an eggsplorer, you can't just stay in the yard all the time."

Good point.

"You need to eggsplore Out West."

Right, like Daniel Boom.

His gaze slid around and landed on me, and a cunning little smile formed on his mouth. "Sometimes my mom takes a nap with my little sister…"

My ears leaped up and I waited for him to finish his thought. He said no more, but gave me a wink that made me wonder if he was thinking what I was thinking he was thinking.

Surely not. His mom had rules about little boys taking a nap in the afternoon, even little boys who wanted to become famous explorers.

I was in the midst of these thoughts when, suddenly and all at once, my ears leaped up into the Full Alert Position. They had just detected a faint rumbling sound in the distance, perhaps a vehicle.

I did a quick check of our Vehicle Log. We had no vehicles scheduled for entry into headquarters at this hour. Slim and Loper had logged out around six o'clock that morning, when they'd gone to work in the field. If you recall, I gave them Escort all the way to the mailbox, then rushed back to my gunny…that is, I returned to the mountain of paperwork on my desk.

Around here, the work never ends.

So it appeared that we had an unauthorized vehicle entering ranch headquarters, and I was the only dog around to work Traffic. (Drover was still hiding in the machine shed). I hit Full Flames on all engines, and went roaring around the north side of the house. There, I began picking up the unauthorized vehicle on instruments.

To be honest, I was a little worried about this Vehicular Intrusion. See, it might have been the mailman, up to something sneaky.   On an average day, he stops at the mailbox on the county road, does something with the box (we're never sure exactly what he's doing), and drives on down the road to the next ranch.

But this promised to be something different. The mysterious vehicle was *heading toward the house.* If that vehicle belonged to the mailman, we might very well find ourselves in the middle of an International Incident that could blow up and spread like wildflowers.

Wildfire, that is, spread like wildfire.

In other words, this could get pretty scary before it gets any scarier. In fact, let me warn you. There's some creepy stuff lying ahead. If you can't handle it...I don't know, go eat a cracker or something and we'll meet on the other side.

CHAPTER SIX

Masked Bandits Rob the Stage Coach

Okay, let's mush on with the story.

There are no ordinary days in the Security Business. The world we inhabit is full of shadows and disguises, spies and imposters, murky characters lurking behind bushes and doing the things we least expect to lease.

A tiny sound in the night might turn out to be a Charlie Monster, and a so-called employee of the Post Office might turn out to be...we never know. That's why we have to put boots on the ground and jets in the sky, and check out everything that looks even slightly suspicious.

I intercepted the vehicle in front of the house and gave it the full load of Halt and Identify Barkings. I was about to disable the tires when...

okay, it was Slim and Loper coming back from the field, and it underscored a point I've made before.

We dogs can't do Traffic Control when our people don't keep up their log books and tell us what's going on.

Maybe it was lunch time and maybe they were coming back for a bite to eat, but how's a dog supposed to know what time it is? Am I a clock? I've never been a clock and I never want to be a clock.

Loper was driving and blew the horn at me. Slim...this was so childish...Slim wrinkled up his face and growled at me through the open window.

I couldn't believe it. Those guys are so... sometimes I get the feeling that they don't take my job seriously. I mean, with them, everything is a big joke.

They didn't deserve an escort, but I ride for the brand and try to do my job. I gave 'em an escort around the south side of the house and up the gravel drive beside the yard gate.

Guess who was sitting beside the gate. Drover. Mister Run and Hide.

I rumbled over to him. He gave me a silly grin and said, "Oh, hi. You're back."

"I'm back and you're in trouble."

"Gosh, what did I do?"

"Disobeying an order, insubordination, cowardice on the field of battle...the list goes on and on. Your court martial will convene at three o'clock and you will probably be fed to the buzzards."

"I saw some buzzards this morning."

"Good. I hope they're hungry."

"It's kind of neat, the way they float in the air like a kite."

"Drover, you're the only dog on this ranch who has time to gawk at buzzards."

"Yeah, 'cause you sleep all the time."

"I do NOT sleep all the time, and let me warn you again about spreading lies and gossip. This will all come out at your court martial. Don't leave the ranch or speak to any strangers."

I marched away and left him sitting in the rubble of his own shubble.

Alfred ran to his dad and they hugged, then went inside to check on the lunch. Slim headed toward the gate and saw me. I was, well, just sitting there, minding my own business.

A grin tugged at one corner of his mouth. "Hankie, when I growled at you, did you think I was the Creature From the Black Latrine? Tell the truth."

Oh brother. No, I did NOT think he was the

Creature From the Whatever It Was. The Black Latrine. And by the way, it was supposed to be the Creature From the Black *Lagoon*. That was the name of a scary movie, but he got it all wrong.

And as for the trick itself...he had pulled that trick so many times, even Drover could have figured it out. It was old, tired, corny, and childish. If he was going to continue this kind of nonsense, at least he could come up with...

Huh?

You won't believe this. I couldn't believe it either. I must have looked away for just a moment, and when I looked back at Slim...he was gone! I'm not kidding, he had vanished, and standing in the spot he had occupied was A TOTAL STRANGER, WEARING A BANDANA OVER HIS NOSE AND MOUTH!

Who wears a mask over his face? Outlaws, that's who, crooks and bandits. Bandits are called "bandits" because they always wear bandanas. See, they put on a mask right before they rob trains and hold up stage coaches, and we had one standing right there beside the yard gate.

A bandit, that is, not a stage coach. We had a masked bandit right in the middle of ranch headquarters!

Where you find one outlaw with a mask, you

can always expect to find several more. They operate in gangs, don't you see, and that's how they pull their jobs. I couldn't see the rest of the crooks, but I knew they were out there somewhere, hiding behind trees and bushes.

Was this scary or what? You bet. It was serious enough to send a buzz of alarm down my backbone and out to the end of my tail. But it got worse. The Masked Bandit raised both hands to shoulder-level and...and the fingers spread apart and...good grief, made CLAWS! Huge creepy claws with talons three inches long...and dripping blood from his last job.

Then he started GROWLING, a rumble from the depths of his throat, hidden somewhere behind the mask. And he began slouching forward...TOWARD ME! It was exactly the kind of stiff-legged slouch you would expect from a masked bandit who had...I don't know, transformed into a monster that eats dogs.

Well, you know me. When monsters show up on the ranch, I don't just sit there, waiting to be torn to shrugs. The hair shot up on my back, and we're talking about every single hair from my ears out to the extremities of my tail section. A gurgling bark took shape in the deeps of my depths, and I began backing way.

And then the creature began uttering some horrible words:

"Fee!

Fie!

Fo!

Fog!

I smell the blood of a dingbat dog!"

Did you hear that? Good grief, he was smelling my blood, and I wasn't even bleeding yet! He kept lurching toward me and I backed away some more, until I backed into my assistant.

"Drover, listen up. You've spent most of your life goofing off, but we need you now."

"It's Slim."

"We're going into Red Alert. Repeat, Red Alert. Form a line, load up Anti-Monster Barks, and go straight into Code Three Procedures."

"It's Slim."

"On my signal, we will lay down a barrage of...what did you say?"

"It's Slim."

I whirled around and gave him a blistering glare. "Are you nuts? I know Slim. I know him very well. I've stayed at his house, slept in his bed, eaten his mackerel sandwiches, and drunk water from his commode. That is not Slim!"

"He's wearing a bandana over his face, is all."

"This has nothing to do with bananas, and I advise you to wipe that monkey grin off your face."

He pointed a paw and widened his silly grin. "Look."

I looked in the direction his paw was pointing and...huh?

Okay, we can relax and call off the Red Alert. You won't believe this. In fact, I don't want to talk about it. I refuse to say another word.

Sorry. I know you're curious, but it's just too outrageous.

Unbelievable.

Shocking.

Okay, I'll talk about it. Do you know the difference between a ranch cowboy and a clown in the carnival? A carnival clown is actually funny, whereas your average cowboy tries to be funny but isn't.

It's pathetic. It's embarrassing. While I'm working eighteen hours a day, trying to run this ranch and keep it safe from whatevers, those guys lie awake at night, thinking of new ways to pull tricks on their dogs.

Loper is bad about it, but Slim is a hundred times worse. The man has no shame. Does he actually do any work on this ranch? Does he get paid for this stuff?

Okay, the Masked Bandit turned out to be Slim. See, he'd tied a red bandana around his face, concealing everything but his eyes, and he did something sneaky with his eyes. I'm not sure what he did, but...

Well, what's a dog to think? One minute we're living in a normal world, on a working cattle ranch with two grown men who pay taxes and have the right to vote, and the next minute, they're playing Clowns and Monsters. How am I supposed to guide the ship when we've got crazy people running through the control room?

Well, as you might expect, Slim enjoyed his little moment of glory. Oh, he loved it! He pulled down the mask and revealed the rest of his face, which consisted mostly of a huge grin. "Did I fool you, pooch?"

I held my head at a proud angle and tried to salvage a few smithers of dignity. I beamed him an icy glare that said, "If your mother could see you today, she would be so ashamed. She'd wonder why she went to all the trouble to raise you."

There, by George, I got him told.

Did he get the message? Of course not. He was too busy laughing at his own stale humor—

just what you'd expect.

You know, if dogs wrote the history books, we would paint a very different picture of the American West, and let me tell you, it would raise some eyebrows.

Just then, Loper stuck his head out the screen door and yelled, "Let's eat! Fried chicken and smashed 'taters."

Slim started toward the gate, but stopped and looked back at me. "Pooch, you're not going to hold a grudge, are you?"

What? Of course I was going to hold a grudge!

"I was just funnin'."

Yeah, well, what's fun for the goose is sauce for the duck.

He patted his thigh with his right hand. "Oh, come 'ere, let's make up and be friends again."

No. He could find himself another friend. Maybe there was a skunk on the ranch who was desperate for companionship. Me? I had better things to do. No.

"Hank, maybe I can smuggle you out some chicken bones."

Bribery would not...chicken bones?

"Now, come on over here and let's make up and be pals again."

Oh, all right. I swallowed my pride, marched

over to him, and collected rubs on the ears and several pats on the ribs. On this outfit, it's always the dogs who end up walking the extra mile, and do you know why? Because dogs CARE about things like loyalty and friendship.

And so it was that Slim and I made a solemn pledge to trudge on with a friendship that he didn't deserve, and he got my friendship at a bargain price. In this world, what else can you buy for a couple of chicken bones?

George Eat
Old Gray Rat

The moment Slim went into the house, I whirled around and marched over to the King of Slackers. "On your feet, soldier, you're going to the brig."

"Me? Gosh, I thought I was going to get a fair trial."

"There's been a change of plans. The case against you is so irremuckable, we don't need to waste time with a fair trial. Let's go."

He whimpered and moaned, but I didn't care. I had been watching his rebellious streak for months. It had started small and had grown and grown, and I couldn't ignore it any longer.

I hate to be severe with the men, but if we don't nip these buds in the nipper, they'll come back to honk us.

I marched the prisoner down to the Security Division's Vast Office Complex. In silence, we rode the elevator up to the twelfth floor—silence, except for his sniffles and whimpers, which I ignored. When the blast-proof door slid open, I led him to his dingy cell and pointed toward the southeast angle-iron leg of the gas tanks.

"You know the routine. Put your nose in the corner."

"Oh drat. For how long?"

"That depends on your attitude. It could take days or weeks. Lately, your attitude has been all over the map."

"Gosh, maybe you could show me the map. I think it would help."

"We don't have a map."

"We could pretend."

I gave that some thought. "I suppose we could. Sure. The imagination is a powerful tool and we should use it to improve our behavior."

"Yeah, that's what I want more than anything, to behave my improver."

"I'm glad to hear you say that, son."

"Thanks, and here's an idea. We can pretend that it's a map of the United Steaks of America."

"The United Steaks?"

"Yeah, 'cause we both love steak."

My tongue shot out and swept across my lips. "Interesting point. We both love steak and the love of knowledge is the beginning of education."

"Yeah, and we'd rather eat a steak than a state."

"Excellent point. Just think of chewing all those trees."

"Yeah, and flag poles. Every state has a flag pole."

"I think you're onto something." I moved to the front of the room and pulled down a huge map of the United Steaks. I tapped my pointer on several spots and plunged into my lecture. "Over here, we have Teebonia, named for the famous steak with a bone in the shape of a T."

"Tee hee. They're great."

"I agree. They're amazing. And over here on the other coast, we have another steak—not the most popular, but still a good, solid choice: Sirloinia."

"Yes sir!"

"And here in the middle, we have Ribeyesylvania. It doesn't have a bone, but make no bones about it, the meat is delicious." There was a moment of silence. "That was a joke, a little humor to liven up our unit on geography."

He gave me a blank stare. "I guess I missed it."

"I said, a rib eye steak has no bone to chew, but make no bones about it, the meat is...never mind. It's probably over your head."

"Yeah, I'm kind of short."

"Exactly. The point we want to take home from this lecture is that geography doesn't have to be a dull and boring subject."

"Yeah, and you're a great teacher."

"Well, thank you. I appreciate...why are you grinning?"

"I just thought of something. You're a great teacher, but I'll bet you can't spell 'geography'."

"Of course I can: jeff-ee-o-graff-graff-y."

He wagged his head from side to side. "Nope, that's wrong."

"All right, it's wrong. I *teach*, but that doesn't mean I can spell. Geography is a huge word, very difficult. No dog in this world could spell it."

"I can."

I paced over to him and looked down into his face. "You? You think you can spell 'geography'? That's crazy."

"Bet me?"

"Drover, I never take unfair advantage of my students."

"The loser has to stand with his nose in the corner for thirty minutes."

"The loser has to...ha ha...this is beyond ridiculous." I paced a few steps away. The runt had caught me by surprise and I wasn't sure...I paced back to him. "Okay, pal, you started this. Let's take it all the way to the finish line. Go for it. Spell 'geography.'"

He sat down, wiggled his stub tail, and squeezed his face into a wad of wrinkles. "George... Eat...Old...Gray...Rat...At...Poppa's...House... Yesterday."

"Yes? And so what? I don't care about George or what he ate. Spell the word."

"I just did, hee hee. You take the first letter of each word and put 'em together: G-E-O-G-R-A-P-H-Y. Geography. Are you proud of me?"

Huh?

We don't need to go into all the details, but let me state for the record that I *wasn't* proud of him. He had used a sneaky trick against one of the few friends he had left in the world, and I, being a trusting soul, had taken the bait.

But let me also hasten to point out that I'm a Dog of My Word. I honor my pledges and pay off my gambling debts, no matter how badly it hurts. And you talk about HURT! You can't imagine the pain I felt when I crept up to that angle-iron leg of the gas tanks, leaned forward, and stuck my nose into the corner.

Nothing in my career with the Security Division had prepared me for such a humildewed experience...such a humilifying experience...such a humiliation, let us say. It was awful. For thirty eternal minutes, I stood there, rubbing a sore on the end of my nose, while Drover hid in some weeds nearby and giggled like a monkey.

I couldn't see the wretch, but I could hear him. "Hee hee hee! I can't believe this. Hank's standing with his nose in the corner! Tee hee hee."

That really cut me to the crick. I mean, you put your heart and soul into helping your men and...phooey.

The good news is that I emerged from the experience a stronger dog, a wiser dog, a dog who had learned a valuable lesson about...something, and it was a very valuable lesson.

The better news was that, at the end of my thirty minutes of torture, Slim came out of the house and yelled, "Hank, come 'ere! Chicken bones!"

I left the dungeon and went sprinting to the yard gate. By the time Slim got there, I was sitting and waiting, a patient, loyal dog, ready to receive his Chicken Bone Reward.

He opened the gate and held up something

wrapped up in a paper napkin. "Are we pals again?"

Oh yes, pals forever!

"Can you catch a bone in the air?"

Does a dog have fleas?

"We'll see." He lifted a chicken leg-bone out of the napkin and held it up. "Okay, pooch, jump-ball."

Bring it on!

He pitched it up into the air. I launched myself and snagged the bone, crunched it up, and rammed it down. Hark, cough, arg! Got a little particle hung in my throat but...hark, gag... sometimes when we eat too fast, we eat too fast.

But I'm no quitter. I cleared the pipes and lined up for the second jump-ball, this time a thigh-bone. It wasn't quite as big or as good as the drumstick, but, by George, I snagged it out of the sky and crunched it up.

Slim watched with a smile. "You do good work, pooch. I guess we'll be pals forever, and I don't have to feel guilty about scaring you out of your drawers."

Right, no problem. Two chicken bones had saved our friendship, and I didn't wear drawers. But let me point out that I hadn't been totally fooled by that business of the Masked Bandit. I had recognized his boots, see, and…well, it's always better to err on the side of caution, right? You bet.

Loper came out on the porch, followed by Little Alfred. They said goodbye and Loper said, "Help your mom and be a good boy, hear?" The kid bobbed his head and said he would, then Loper joined Slim at the gate. "Well, back to the field. Radio says the rain chances are looking good."

"Sure would be a good day for a nap."

"Sleep on the tractor."

"What if I fall off and get run over?"

"I've always thought you'd make good fertilizer. You're not good for much else."

Slim laughed. "You know, when I hired onto this outfit, somebody said it was going to be a *cowboy* job."

"Naw. That was just bait for the gullible."

"It sure was. Nobody said a word about driving a piece-of-junk tractor fourteen hours a day. That thing's so noisy, I'm going deaf."

"Wear ear plugs."

"I ain't got any."

"Spit wads work fine."

"Made out of what?"

"A bolt sack."

"What about my chapped lips?"

"You've got a grease gun."

"My lips are so raw, I can't hardly smile."

"Guud. The boss always worries when the hired hands are smiling. You drive." Loper went to the passenger-side of the pickup.

"How come?"

"I'm going to take a nap on the way to the field. You can blabber all you want and I won't hear a thing."

Slim shook his head and climbed behind the wheel. "Loper, if they ever did heart surgery on you, they'd find a lead brick. They'd have to cut into it with a diamond-tipped saw."

He started the pickup and off they went to the field. Slim was still talking, but Loper stuck his fingers in his ears, scooted down in the seat, and closed his eyes.

Well! At last we had some peace and quiet. I mean, those two could go on like that for hours at a time, yapping at each other and never solving anything. But the silence didn't last long. Just as the pickup disappeared, I heard Sally May's voice calling from inside the house.

"Alfred? Honey, it's time for your nap."

I turned and looked at the boy. I expected to see a big frown on his face, because...well, he hated naps. But this time, he flashed a mysterious little grin, winked at me and said, "I'll see you in a little bit. We're gonna eggsplore!"

Hmm. I had a feeling that this might lead us into troubled waters, so to speak, but I had no idea...well, you'll see. We ended up in troubled waters For Real.

Keep reading.

I Have No
Use For A Nap

I understand why kids hate naps. There's so much to do in the world, so many things going on out there, and so little time to do them before the sun goes down, yet after lunch, in the middle of the day, they have to stop everything, go to their rooms, lie down, and sleep for an hour.

What a bummer. Yes, I understand these kids and I pretty muchly have the same opinion about nap-taking. I have no use for a nap in the middle of the day.

On the other hand...well, it's a little different when you're Head of Ranch Security. We spend most of our time at the top of the mountain, don't you see, and you know how it is up there: high altitude, thin air, low levels of carbon diego, and the crushing weight of responsibility that never ends.

Just think about it. We have to put up with mouthy cats and people who don't understand the kind of work we do. Half the time, they're yelling at us and chasing us with brooms, and the other half, they're playing silly tricks on us.

Then we have to worry about the staff. When you have employees, it's like living in a house infested with mice. You walk out of the room and they start taking the place apart. I won't mention any names.

Yes I will. Drover. Remember that deal about spelling "geography"? It was crooked from the start. The little mutt couldn't even spell "cat," but he'd schemed a way of luring me into a trap, see, and the longer I thought about it, the thoughter it made me.

You might have missed this little detail, but our whole purpose for going down to the gas tanks had been to stick HIS nose in the corner, but somehow he managed to...

Phooey. The point is that all this stuff wears on a dog, drags him down, and warpens his spirit, and once in a great while, the thought of taking a nap in the middle of the day seems...well, not so bad.

In fact, there are times when a dog mutts realize that he can swerve his ranch bets when he turks care ot his snork...takes care of his health. And getting adequate skonk is a very impecking park of the piddle. An important part of the process.

Sorry, I'm getting a little drowsy.

Anyway, I really hated the idea of putting my sniggle...pudding my schedule on hold for an hour, but I marched my snickerdoodles...I marched myself down to the office, turned off all the phones, and curled up on my gummy snick bug...my gunny sack bed.

The ranch needed for me to get my rest. No kidding.

Wow, what a great bed! That gunny sack and I had been through some hard times and we had become the bonk of friends. Within smeckonds, I dribbled out on the snee of calm molasses and purple zebras floated past in rubber tubbies. Honking sassafras twerping turnip tops and murgle skiffer pork chop snizzle whurping saw horses in the whooping crane palace, while George ate old gray rats at poppa's house yesterday.

Zzzzzzzzzzzzzzzzzzzzzzzzzzzzzzzzzzzzzzzzzz zzzzz.

My first clue that I wasn't standing in the Whooping Crane Palace came when I heard...was that a voice? Yes, a voice, calling my name.

"Hank? You'd better wake up."

With great effort, I began cranking up the shade on my left eye. I saw...gee, this was strange...I saw a purple zebra floating past in a rubber tubby. No, wait, it might have been a dog. Yes, a smallish dog with a ridiculous stub tail.

I cranked up the shade on my other eye and saw the same dog I'd seen with the first eye. I'd never seen this guy before.

"Hank, you'd better wake up. Little Alfred's calling you."

I staggered to my feet and rushed into the control room and found chaos—lights flashing, smoke pouring out of the control panel, gongs gonging. I began flipping switches and spoke to the stranger.

"All is lost! We must lower the lifeboats. Don't just stand there, we're going down! Wait. Who are you anyway?"

"I'm Drover, the same Drover who woke you up the last time."

"Good. We'll be sharing a lifeboat, so let me warn you. Eating old gray rats in my boat will not be tolerated." He started laughing. "You

75

think this is funny? We've lost the ship and all you can think about is eating rats! What's wrong with you?"

"Hank, it's not a ship and we're not going down."

"You talk as though we've met before."

"Ten thousand times. You were asleep... again."

"How dare you say that? I ought to have you..." I blinked my eyes and glanced around. "Wait. It's all coming back. Don't you get it? I must have dozed off."

"Duh."

"And you're Drover. All right, we're cooking now. Bring me up to speed. What's going on around here?"

"Little Alfred's calling you."

"He's the boy, right? Go on."

"He's calling you from his bedroom window."

"You don't suppose he's eating old gray rats, do you?" Drover rolled his eyes and began pounding on his head with a paw. "Stop that. You look ridiculous."

"Hank, let's go see what he wants."

"I'll give the orders around here." I took a gulp of fresh air and tried to clear my head. "Okay, let's go see what he wants. To the house!"

We left the office with a blast of fire and jet fumes, and went streaking toward the house. By then, it was clear that I had dozed off, and that explained some of the confusion, but I never did figure out why Drover had been eating rats.

What can you say? He's a weird little mutt.

We arrived at the yard fence thirty seconds after lift-off, cut the engines, and coasted to a smooth landing. I glanced around and saw nothing and nobody. But then I heard a voice coming from the house. It said, "Pssst! Hankie, over here."

I didn't dare dive over the fence and enter the yard, but trotted around the outside of the fence and stopped on the south side. There, I had a clear view of the house, including Little Alfred's bedroom window. He had raised the window and was waving at me through the screen.

"Hi, Hankie. You want to sneak into my room?"

Sneak into his room? Ha ha. We didn't need to discuss that form of suicide. No.

His face sank into a scowl. "Welp, I guess I could sneak outside and we could go eggsploring."

Hmm. I had a feeling his mother might not approve of that.

"My mom's taking a nap."

Yeah, but what about Mommy Radar? It could pick up a mouse walking around in ballet slippers, two miles away.

"I don't think she'd mind, Hankie."

I wasn't so sure about that.

Drover had arrived by that time. I turned to him. "Did you hear what he said?"

"Who?"

"Little Alfred, who else? He's thinking of sneaking outside."

Drover's eyes grew wide with alarm. "During naptime?"

"Roger that. He's got this idea in his head about becoming a famous explorer."

"I don't think that's a good idea."

"I agree. We'll tell him that his dogs have considered the matter and we think..." But it was too late to spill the milk. Little Alfred tip-toed out the door, wearing a devilish little grin.

Drover began backing away. "You know, I need to go check out some things in the machine shed. See you later."

I blocked his path and gave him a withering glare. "You will NOT go hide in the machine shed. You've spent your whole life being a little weenie and it's time for you to grow up."

"Yeah, but..."

"Drover, we're responsible for the children. It's one of the most important parts of our job."

"Yeah, but...even when they're naughty?"

"Especially when they're naughty. Naughty little boys need the good influence of their dogs. Who else cares about them as much as we do?"

"Gosh, I never thought about it that way. We really do care, don't we?"

"With all our hearts."

His eyes seemed to be filling with tears. "It's so sweet...a boy and his dogs. It almost makes me want to cry."

You probably think that Drover and I had ourselves a nice little cry, thinking about the bond of love between dogs and little boys. Ha. Not so fast. Here's a tiny detail you might have missed, because, well, you weren't there. But I was there and I picked it up right away.

See, there was something fishy about Drover's emotional so-forth. While he seemed to be fighting back tears, he was also *backing away from me*. Do you see a familiar pattern here? It was leading toward his usual response to Life Itself. If I hadn't blocked his path again, he would have high-balled it straight to his Secret Sanctuary.

As I've said before, it's not that I don't trust

Drover. It's that he can't be trusted.

I blocked his path, stuck my nose in his face, and gave him some fangs. "You little weasel, don't even think about running away."

He keeled over and began kicking all four legs at once. "He's a little brat and he's going to get us in trouble!"

"He might be a little brat, but he's OUR little brat."

"Sally May will screech at us!"

"Then so be it. It's just part of the job."

"I hate exploring, it hurts my feet!"

"Nobody cares. You *will* go on this mission and you *will* do your job."

He struggled to his feet and you can't imagine how pitiful he looked, limping and dragging himself along. If I had never seen this kind of performance before, it might have touched my heart, but I had seen it so many times, it didn't come close to touching my heart. It didn't even touch my toes.

Besides, by that time, Little Alfred was standing beside us. His eyes were sparkling. "Come on, doggies, wet's go eggsplore!"

And so the adventure began.

Our Vocabulary
Lesson For Today

Before we plunge into the spooky part of this story, maybe we should pause a moment and have Our Vocabulary Lesson For Today. See, most stories are made up of *words*. In fact, all stories are made up of words. Without words, stories would consist of dozens of empty pages, which would make them hard to read and very boring. Without words, we would all be speechless.

Hencely, it's important that we stay on top of this business of translating Kid Language into forms of speech that the rest of us can understand. In our previous lesson, we discussed "twucks" and the true meaning of "eggsplore." After a few false starts, we figured out that "eggsploring" has nothing to do with eggs, no matter how they're cooked or whether they're served with bacon, slurp, sausage, or hash browns.

Now we're ready to translate another of Little Alfred's vocabulary words: "wet's." In Kid Language, "wet's" means "let's." It could also be translated as "let us" or "lettuce," but not as "cabbage." Dogs have no interest in cabbage.

Come to think of it, we have no interest in lettuce either. We love MEAT, so let's just skip the vegetables.

Okay, when the lad said, "Wet's go eggsploring," the correct translation comes out as, "Let us go exploring."

And here are your vocabulary words for today. "Twuck" means "truck," "Wet" means "let," "burfessional" means "professional," and "eggsplore" means "explore." Write those definitions twenty times before bedtime and don't forget to brush your teeth.

Is this neat or what? You bet. I get a thrill out of messing around with words. And I'll tell you something else. I can give you a secret formula that will allow you to spell a word that is almost impossible to remember how to spell the spelling of which.

Check this out:

George
Ate
Three
Blind
Mice
At
Grandma's
House
Yesterday.

Are you still with me? Here's the secret part. You take the first letter of each word, put 'em all together, and you get the correct spelling. Okay, let's write the word on the blackboard. This is so cool! You'll love it.

GATBMAGHY.

Wait. That doesn't look right. I mean, GATBMAGHY is not a word, at least not in this solar system. Hmm. Perhaps we...phooey. Let's skip the vocabulary lesson and mush on with the story.

If you recall, Little Alfred had just sneaked out of his room, out of the house, and out of the yard, and was fixing to launch himself into a new career as a Famous Explorer. And Drover and I were aware that this was a violation of his

mother's Plan For Little Boys.

Alfred was supposed to take a nap during Naptime.

Alfred was not supposed to sneak out of the house and run wild.

We dogs were fully aware of the risks involved in joining his expedition (we might get blamed), but as the Elite Troops of the Security Division, we had sworn a solemn oath to protect the little children from harm and danger.

And, fellers, when a dog takes an oath, he's oathed for life.

Bottom Line: We weren't about to let that kid run loose on the ranch without the supervision of two loyal dogs—or, to put it more accurately, without the supervision of one loyal dog and one little ninny who wanted to hide in the machine shed, only I had put a whoa to that.

GATBMAGHY. It worked just fine for Mister Smartypants. I don't get it.

Anyway, Little Alfred had escaped from his room and there we were, standing outside the yard. He looked us over and said, "Are y'all ready to go eggsploring?"

Locked and loaded.

"We won't go far and we'll get back before my mom wakes up."

Good.

"Should we take Pete?"

What? Take the cat on an important expedition? Absolutely not! Kitty was too lazy, too fat, too selfish, and too much of a conniving little hickocrip to go exploring with us. The last thing we needed on our adventure was a cat.

Alfred must have come to the same conclusion. "Nah. He's too much trouble."

Exactly right. Good boy!

"Come on, doggies! Follow me."

Onward! We followed him around to the yard

gate on the west side of the house. There, he pointed to his red Western Flyer wagon. "Okay, y'all, we're going Out West in my covered wagon."

For some reason, Drover happened to be listening and his ears perked up. "Hey, did you hear that? We get to ride in the wagon. Oh goodie."

"Sounds like fun, doesn't it?"

"Oh yeah. I've never ridden in a wagon before."

"Neither have I. This could turn out to be…"

Huh? Wait a second. All three of us couldn't ride in the wagon. Someone had to pull it, right? Hmmm. My mind began expanding in all directions, and a clever plan began to form.

I leaned toward Drover and whispered, "Remember that little promotion we've been talking about? I just had a great idea. How would you like to volunteer to pull the wagon?"

"Oh, I'd rather ride."

"Drover, anyone can ride in a wagon. It takes a special kind of dog to pull one."

"Yeah, but you're bigger than me."

"That's my whole point. The bigger we are, the more we need to share the opportunities."

"Yeah, but I'm just a runt."

"Drover, that's exactly what I'm saying. The

runter you are, the harder you must work to overcome your runtness."

"Gosh, you really think I could do it?"

"No question about it. It would build your confidence and give you some valuable experience."

He thought about that, and, you know, for the first time in months, I detected a spark of ambition in his eyes. "Maybe you're right. Maybe I can do it."

"Son, you can do it. You just have to believe in yourself."

He lifted his head to a proud angle. "I think I can do it."

"That's the spirit!"

"But I'd better warm up this old leg."

"Good thinking, and I'll give you some coaching tips."

This was working out better than I had dared to hope. Drover would gain valuable experience, working as a draft horse, and I would gain even more valuable experience, watching him do it—whilst riding in the wagon. Hee hee.

What a deal, huh?

Westward Ho the Wagons!

You know who gets to ride around in wagons, don't you? Caesars, pharaohs, kings, emperors, honored guests, and Heads of Ranch Security. Those of us who live at the top of the mountaintop have our little privileges, don't you see, and when someone throws a parade, you won't find us pulling wagons.

I had been chosen to ride in an open carriage, while Drover had volunteered to be Nag of the Day. Everything had fallen into place, almost as though someone had...well, planned it that way.

In fact, someone had. ME. In case you didn't notice, I had employed several clever tricks to boost his confidence and coax him into becoming a helpful little doggie, instead of his usual slacker-self.

It's called Lordship. Wait. It's called Leadership. We inspire the men to push their limits and accomplish impossible foots. You don't rise to the rank of Head of Ranch Security without developing those crucial Leadership Skills.

All that remained was for me to give the mutt a little dab of coaching and, you know, help him get his muscles tuned up for the big job ahead.

"All right, son, step out. Pick 'em up and lay 'em down. Lift those legs as high as you can and let's get those Upper Boogaloo muscles stretched out. This is going to be a very important assignment."

Remember that little spark of ambition I had noticed in his eyes? Well, I was pleased to see that it had grown into something bigger, more of a glow than a spark. The little guy was responding to my coaching and was rising to face one of the biggest challenges of his whole career. And I must admit that it made me proud.

He moved his legs up and down and rolled his shoulders. "Boy, it's all coming together. I can feel it. This is going to be my big day!"

"Looking good, son. Practice your starts."

"I'm on it." He crouched down in a sprinter's stance and yelled, "Here I go!"

Wow. He sprang out of the blocks like an

arrow shot out of a canon and...huh? There was a clattering sound, a thump, a cloud of dust, and...I couldn't believe this. He went down like a load of hay, and came up...limping.

"Oh rats, there it went! This old leg just quit me! Oh, my leg!"

For a moment, I was too shocked to speak, then I managed to yell, "Drover, stop acting like a little..."

Too late. Alfred had been watching the whole thing and now he was shaking his head. "I don't think Drover would make a very good horse. He's too much of a shrimp."

Exactly right. He was a shrimp, but even worse, he was a shrimp with a devious mind.

Guess who got tagged for the Horse Detail. Me. While Drover limped and groaned, Alfred rigged me with a piece of cotton rope and harnessed me to the wagon. My face burned with anger and disappointment. My coaching career had gone down in flames, along with my hopes of riding in a parade in an open carriage.

It almost broke my heart. Leadership is wasted when you're surrounded by ninnies.

The boy got me harnessed to the wagon, stepped back and gave me a looking over. "Hankie, you're gonna make a good horse, 'cause you're so big and strong."

Big and strong? That was true, of course. Yes. I had a pretty amazing set of shoulders and have we ever discussed my legs? Wow. You talk about a pair of awesome legs! Powerful, and we're talking about muscles that are like steel springs.

As I've always said, it isn't every dog that gets chosen to pull a covered wagon Out West. It's a very special honor and it doesn't go to just any old mutt that needs a job.

So, yes, it was a proud moment for me, for the ranch, for the entire Security Division. Out of all the dogs in the world, I had been chosen to pull my little pal's wagon on an exciting adventure, exploring the Wild West.

Alfred climbed into the wagon and it didn't bother me that he invited the King of Slackers to ride with him. Okay, it bothered me, but not for long, and here's why. Do you know who rides around in wagons? The shrimps and the half-steppers. I say, "Let 'em have it." It takes a *real* dog to pull a wagon.

I also took some comfort in knowing that this would all come out at Drover's next court martial.

Well, we were all set for our trek Out West. When Alfred gave me the command to move out ("Gitty Up"), I leaned into the harness like a giant locomotive and began lugging the wagon.

No ordinary dog could have pulled such a load. Me? I hardly even noticed. Piece of cake.

You know, the funny thing about our trip Out West was that...well, we headed south, not west. That seems odd, doesn't it? Alfred chose the

route because the terrain south of the house was flat and smooth, better suited for wagon traffic.

In the Real World, if you're heading Out West, you probably ought to go west, but when kids and dogs are running the show, it really doesn't matter. By George, Out West can be anywhere we want it to be, and on that particular day, it lay south of the house.

And so our journey began. On and on we pushed—over mountain passes that were still clogged with snow, across mighty rivers with steamboats chugging past, across burning deserts where the only living things we saw were cactus trees and two-hump camels.

It must have been somewhere in the middle of the desert that we made a sad discovery. Our horse was getting tired, and we're talking about bleary-eye, tongue-dragging, gasping-for-air kind of tired. The grand adventure that had begun as a piece of cake had turned into a piece of something quite a bit heavier than cake, maybe bricks or lead weights.

Gag, I was bushed, and you know what really hurt? We hadn't gone more than a hundred feet from the house, for crying out loud.

The Wagon Boss tried to urge me on. "Come on, horsie, gitty up! Gitty up!"

Gitty Up was out of the question. It was time for me to Gitty Down, and that's what I did. I sat down, unrolled about six inches of tongue, and went into our Maximum Ventilation Program (panting for air).

Alfred was disappointed. I could see it all over his face. "Hankie, we're not there yet."

Yeah, well, we were as "there" as we were likely to get for a while. I had to take a break and refill my tanks with...

Huh?

You won't believe this. Would you like to guess who showed up at that very moment, and I mean out of nowhere, like flies at a picnic? I'll give you some hints.

Hint #1: He wasn't invited.

Hint #2: He wasn't invited because nobody could stand his company.

Hint #3: He came slithering up behind me and began rubbing on my left front leg.

Hint #4: He flicked the end of his tail across my nose.

Did you figure it out? It was Mister Never Sweat, Sally May's rotten little cat, and for reasons I could not imagine, he had left the yard and hiked out into the pasture to join us.

I pushed him away. "Get that tail out of my

face. What are you doing out here, you little creep?"

"Now Hankie, don't be that way. You might not believe this, but I've come to help."

A jagged laugh leaped out of my throat. "Help? You? The last time you helped, you helped yourself to my scraps."

His eyes lit up. "You know, I did, and they were delicious. But, Hankie, this is different." He stared at me with his mysterious kitty eyes. "I really do think I can help you."

I ran this through Data Control. He was up to some kind of trickery, but I couldn't figure it out. "Okay, I'll bite. Help me what?"

"I can help you pull the wagon."

"You can help me...ha ha! Oh, that's rich, that's hilarious. You couldn't even pull an empty bean can, much less a wagon."

He rolled over on his back and began playing with his tail. "Well, it all depends on how you approach it, Hankie. You should look for your Hidden Strength. Scissors cut paper. Rock breaks scissors. Paper covers rock."

"Yeah, and dog runs kitty up a tree. So what?"

His face bloomed with a smile. "That's it, Hankie, you figured it out!"

"I did?"

"Yes, and I am just amazed. You discovered

your Hidden Strength, based on a law of physics."

"I don't get it."

He sat up and lowered his voice to a whisper. *"A dog is never too tired to chase a cat."*

"Wait a second. Are you saying..."

"I'll hiss, you'll chase. In chasing, you'll pull the wagon and entertain the child."

My mind was swirling. I would have begun pacing, as I often do in such swirling situations, but, well, I was hitched to the wagon.

"Okay, Pete, let's go straight to the bottom line. What's in it for you? And don't give me any baloney about how you care about me or Little Alfred or anyone else on this planet, because I know you don't."

He fluttered his eyes and studied his paw. "Hankie, I...am...bored."

I stared at him in amazement. "You're *bored*? You're so bored that you want me to chase you?"

His eyes crackled with delight and he nodded his head. "Yes, and I think it might turn out to be fun."

This was one of the craziest things I'd ever heard, and the craziest part was that...it might actually work.

CHAPTER ELEVEN

Prisoners in a Cave

It almost made me ill that Pete had come up with a solution to our Energy Crisis, and that I hadn't. It was so simple yet so true.

A dog is never too tired to chase a cat.

"Okay, Pete, I've run the numbers and it might work."

"You're welcome, Hankie."

"I didn't say 'thank you.'"

"I know. That would hurt, wouldn't it?"

"More than you can imagine. Let's get started. Anything for the kids."

"Very well, Hankie. Stand by for blast-off."

Kitty took his position right in front of me, and we're talking about nose-to-nose. He flattened his ears and threw a hump into his back. The pupils of his eyes became large black circles and he cranked up the yowling sound that is sure to build a fire in the mind of a dog.

It worked. I felt a rush of thermonuclear energy, and the engines of my mind began to roar and tremble with an incredible force. Over the roar and rumble, I heard the countdown coming from Mission Control: "Three, two, one..."

Kitty hit the Launch Button. He HISSED right in my face and smacked me across the nose with his claws. Ouch. That did it! The world went red and the chase was on!

You talk about a blast-off! Drover did a back flip over the back end of the wagon and landed on the ground. Little Alfred grabbed the sides and held on for dear life. Kitty went streaking south, toward the creek, and I was in hot pursuit, blasting him with enormous barks and trying to snap off the end of his tail.

Behind me, I heard Alfred scream, "Hankie, no! Wait, stop!"

Too late. There was no turning back now. The weapon had been launched and Sir Figgy Newton was driving the bus.

Sir Isaac Newton, I guess it should be, the famous scientist. In other words, we had uncorked a bottle of Pure Physics.

The earth rushed past me and the next thing I knew, we had run out of flat prairie country and, up ahead, I saw the brushy undergrowth along the creek. A tiny voice inside my head whispered a warning: "Don't go crashing into the brush."

Yeah, well, that was a nice idea, but somehow it didn't register. When you mess around with the laws of figgies...the laws of physics...anyway, we went crashing into a bunch of tamaracks and came to a sudden stop.

The wagon and I had gotten high-centered in the brush, is the point. I was gasping for air. Alfred's mouth hung open and his eyes were wide with...I don't know, surprise, fear, or excitement, I suppose. I had given him a pretty wild ride.

I needed help but saw no sign of Kitty. "Hey Pete, front and center!" He took his sweet time, of course. Cats always do that and it drives me nuts, but I must admit that I was kind of glad when he came slithering through a crack in the brush. "There you are. Good. Listen, pal, we have a little problem."

He swept his gaze over the scene. "Not a little problem, Hankie."

"Okay, a big problem. How are you at untying knots?"

"Well, Hankie, cats don't do knots." He gazed

up at the sky. "And cats don't do *wet* either."

"What does wet have to do with anything?"

He pointed a paw toward the north. "Rain."

I turned my head around and saw...gulp. A huge gray wall of clouds was moving toward us from the northwest. Lightning flashed and I heard the sound of thunder.

A storm was heading our way, and fellers, it

was BIG and UGLY, one of the scariest storms I'd seen in years.

"Hey Pete, we need to get the boy back to the house, and I was wondering…"

He began edging away. "We need to get *the cat* back to the house, Hankie. I'm not bored any longer, and I hate getting wet. Bye now, and good luck."

"Pete, wait. You can't just…come back here, you little traitor!"

He was gone, poof, and I shouldn't have been surprised. When you're in trouble, don't call a cat.

I turned to my little pal. The thunder was getting louder now, and he looked as scared as I felt. "What are we gonna do, Hankie?"

I used my tail to tap out a message. "It appears that we're going to get drenched, pelted with hailstones, and possibly blown away in a tornado. If the creek comes up, we'll get swept away in a flood. If we happen to survive all of that, your mother will paddle your little behind and flog me with her mop."

Maybe that was the wrong message. His lip began to quiver and a tear slid down his cheek. "Hankie, I want to go home."

I tapped out another message. "So do I. Let's see if we can get out of this mess. You can start by untying the rope."

He seemed to understand. He swiped the tears away with his hand, crawled out of the wagon, and started working on the knot. The thunder was getting louder. His hands were shaking. Hurry up! By this time, I could hear the roar of the wind and rain. I glanced off to the north and saw the house disappear behind a wall of gray.

At last he got the knot untied, just as the storm hit us, and boy, did it hit us! The wind screamed in the cottonwood trees, and all at once it was raining snakes, weasels, and pitchforks, raining so hard, we could hardly breathe.

The world went dark. We couldn't see and had no sense of direction. Together, we stumbled through tamaracks and willows, two tiny souls lost in a raging storm.

And I'm afraid we're going to have to stop right here. The story has gotten out of control and...well, you know me. I worry about the children. I don't mind giving them some scary stuff once in a while, but this...it might be too much. No kidding.

Don't whine. You think you can handle scary stuff, but you don't know what's coming.

What do you say we just shut everything

down, brush our teeth, and climb into a nice warm bed? We can crawl under the covers and snuggle up and...

You want to keep going? Okay, you asked for it. Hang on, here we go.

Okay, two lost souls in the so-forth. We staggered and stumbled. The wind screamed, the thunder roared, and we began hearing the thud of hailstones striking the trees around us. Big stones, the kind that can hurt a little boy. But then...

A bird was standing on the ground in front of us. An owl. Holy smokes, it was Madame Moonshine, and she yelled over the storm, "My goodness, look what I've found. Quick! Follow me, tally-ho!"

I'm not the kind of dog who makes a habit of following owls to unknown places, in the middle of howling storms, but, well, I had run out of ideas.

We followed her across a shallow spot in the creek and kept her in sight as she hopped and flapped toward her cave in the south bank of the creek. Slipping and sliding in the mud, we made our way up the embankment, where she stood, pointing a wing toward the opening.

She called out, "Timothy, open the outer gates!" At that moment, a big hailstone whacked her on top of the head. She turned an angry glare toward the sky and shook her wing. "And YOU will cease striking me with stones!" Another one beaned her on the nose. She rubbed her beak, muttered something, turned to us, and yelled, "Hurry, scurry, in the cave/Never worry, ever brave!"

We dived into the cave—not quite "ever brave," but safe from the storm.

Whew! I had been in this cave before, you know, long away and far ago. This was the cave where Madame Moonshine had cured me of a terrible case of Eye-Crosserosis. Remember that deal? The place hadn't changed much—a fairly large cave with mouse bones scattered across the floor and long tree roots hanging from the ceiling.

Little Alfred took it all in with wide, wondering eyes, and moved closer to me.

Madame hopped past us and stood on a little raised platform at the front. She clasped her wings together, leaned forward, and studied me with her big full-moon eyes. "You're an odd-looking rabbit. Haven't we met?"

"Yes ma'am, this very morning. I'm Hank the Cowdog. Remember me?"

"Yes, of course, but why do you keep telling everyone that you're a rabbit?"

"I've never told anyone that I'm a rabbit."

"You're ashamed of it, aren't you?"

"No ma'am, I'm not a rabbit."

"If you insist you're not a rabbit, then why are you so ashamed of being a rabbit? It seems irrational. You can't go though life being ashamed of what you're not." She closed her eyes and seemed to be lost in thought. "Had you ever thought of being a woodpecker?"

I didn't mean to laugh, but it jumped out. "Ha ha. No ma'am, I've never thought of that."

Her eyes popped open. "Please don't laugh. There is nothing silly about being a woodpecker. Every woodpecker on this ranch is proud of himself, and you'll never find one that goes around claiming to be a rabbit."

"Yes ma'am, sorry."

She shook her head and gazed up at the roots on the ceiling. "Something about this doesn't make sense."

"I agree, so maybe we can change the subject. When the rain stops, I need to get this boy back home."

Her eyes drifted down to me. "Home? Oh, I'm afraid that isn't possible. We're having too much fun. I don't get many visitors, you know. Timothy? Close the outer doors! Raise the draw-bridge and secure the walls."

Uh oh. Remember Big Tim? He was Madame Moonshine's pet rattlesnake and personal bodyguard. We hadn't seen him when we'd come into the cave, but we saw him now. He was coiled up in the door, rattling his tail and flicking out his long black tongue.

Gulp. Unless I was badly mistaken, we had just become prisoners in Madame Moonshine's cave. This wasn't what I'd had in mind.

Pretty spooky, huh? You bet. But we have to keep going. Hang on.

There we were, prisoners in Madame Moonshine's cave, with a six-foot diamondback rattlesnake guarding the door. Little Alfred was one scared little boy and held me tight, and I must admit that I was a little nervous too.

I had just carried on a loony conversation with the owner of the cave, and we're talking about LOONY. The only thing she'd said that made any sense was, "This doesn't make any sense." Where do you go from there?

Nowhere. The conversation dropped dead and for a long time, we sat there, hostages inside a gloomy cave. While the storm raged outside, Madame Moonshine entertained us with tricks. She balanced a mouse bone on the end of her beak and showed us how she could swivel her head around backwards.

I thought it was kind of boring, to tell you the truth, but she seemed to be having the time of her life. But then...hmm. I noticed that the rain had stopped...and thought of something I should have thought of sooner.

"Hey Madame, do you remember knocking yourself out on a window this morning?"

She stopped in the middle of her trick and gave me a puzzled look. "This morning? Oh, that was years ago."

"It was hours ago. You saw your reflection in the window and thought it was another bird."

She scowled and stroked her chin with the tip of her wing. "Now that you mention it...yes, it's coming back. There was a woodpecker on the other side of the glass. Was that you? Yes, of course! So you really ARE a woodpecker! I knew we'd met before."

Oh brother.

"No ma'am, you saw your reflection in the glass and whammed into it."

"I did that? How silly."

"It knocked you out. You fell to the ground, and a cat was about to eat you."

"Hmm, yes, it's coming back now. So...you

were the cat?"

"I was the dog who kept the cat from eating you."

"I thought you were a rabbit."

"I'm a dog!"

She seemed bewildered. "Oh my, this is confusing. So...did anyone eat me?"

"No ma'am, I saved your life."

She smiled and blinked her eyes. "Of course, and that's why I'm still here! You know, I've been wondering about that all day, and the answer is...I'm here because nobody ate me this morning." She began pacing. "But there's more to this, isn't there? Did I make any promises?"

"You sure did. You said that my good deed would come back to me as a blessing."

She stopped pacing and stared at the floor. "I did say that, I know I did. So now...you want to collect?"

"Right, exactly. I need to get this boy back home."

Her voice dropped into a creepy whisper. "Very well, but only if you can answer The Ominous Riddle of Fog, and I must warn you, it is very, very difficult."

Gulp.

CHAPTER TWELVE

The Ominous
Riddle of Fog

There was a long moment of silence. Then Madame swiveled her head around. "Do you wish to continue?"

"What if I get the wrong answer?"

Her gaze roamed the ceiling. "Oh, please don't."

"Pretty bad?"

"Never has anyone who unfailed the test not managed to unsurvive."

"Uh...say that again."

"No one in the entire universe has ever not managed to unsurvive a non-passing score of more than three but less than one."

"So...if I score a two, I'll be okay?"

"If you score a two, you will transform into a

purple penguin. Are you prepared to risk it?"

I swallow a lump in my throat. "Sure. Let's give it a shot."

"Foolish rabbit, wiser penguin." She faced me with a solemn owlish expression. "Pencils up! You have thirty seconds to do the calculations. Here is your test question. If Peter Piper picked a peck of pickled okra, how much wood would a chipmunk chip, if a chipmunk would chip wood? Begin calculating!"

Good grief! I didn't have much time for this, so I cranked up all the resources of Data Control, and we plunged into heavy-duty math. The machines clicked and whirred as I threw myself into the task. I had just arrived at an answer when her voice ripped through the silence.

"Time! Pencils down! Your solution?"

In a shaky voice, I delivered my answer. "Twenty-three ricks of wood and thirteen jars of pickled okra."

She flinched in surprise. "Astounding. But what kind of wood?"

"Hackberry."

"Green or cured?"

"Cured."

"Split or round?"

"Round. No, wait, split."

"And the okra? Does it take the form of okra pickles or pickled okra?"

"Uh...both, half and half."

"With or without a clove of garlic?"

"With garlic."

"Pint jars or quarts?"

"Pints."

Her jaw dropped. "Unbelievable! No one has come close to solving that riddle, yet you did it in mere seconds."

"So...I passed? No kidding?"

"Not only passed, but scored a perfect minus-three hundred. Has anyone ever said that you might be a genius?"

I almost fainted with relief. "Well, I don't want to brag, but...yes ma'am, I hear that quite a lot."

"I'm sure you do." She cupped a wing around her beak. "Timothy! Open the outer gates and let the prisoners leave. And don't you dare hiss at them!"

Big Tim slithered out of his coils and cleared the opening, but he didn't look too happy about it. He gave us the old Pit Viper Glare and continued flicking out his tongue. We hurried past him.

Only then did I feel secure enough to say, "You need to keep that thing in your mouth, buddy, or somebody's liable to step on it."

Hee hee. That was fun, mouthing off to a snake, but the fun didn't last long. The moment we stepped out of the cave, we heard an odd rushing sound. The rain had stopped, but the creek was running hard, fast, and bank-to-bank.

Madame had walked outside with us. "Madame, I don't suppose you know any magic words that would help us cross the creek, do you?"

"No. Yes. Well, maybe. Let me think." She pressed the tips of her wings against her head and closed her eyes.

"Oh, vapors, vapors, vanilla wafers.
Crocodiles and eagle beaks.
Reveal to us a magic word
To help them cross the flooded creek."

Her eyes popped open and she beamed a smile. "It came, I've got it! But you must never share the secret word with anyone. Promise?"

I raised my right front paw. "You have my Solemn Cowdog Oath."

"Very well." She crept closer and dropped her voice to an eerie whisper. "The secret, solemn, magic word is...HELP!"

"Help? That's not a magic word."

She gave me a wink. "Try it. Goodbye, O Rabbity Hank, and come again some time!"

And with that, she hopped back into her cave and Big Tim closed the gates behind her, so to speak.

Alfred and I made our way down to the creek and found it running wide and swift. Most dogs would have quit right there. I mean, we're talking about a flood. But don't forget, Madame had given me the magic word that would...I don't know, pick us up and carry us across to the other side, I suppose. Isn't that what magic words are supposed to do?

At the water's edge, I took a wide stance, grabbed a big gulp of air, and barked the magic word. "HELP!" We waited and listened. Nothing happened, so I reloaded and blasted it out again, over and over, for a solid minute.

And nothing happened, except that I got a sore throat.

You know, with Madame Moonshine, a guy can never be sure if she's totally weird, partly weird, or something in between. On this deal, her magic word had turned out to be a big flop.

Alfred was getting restless. "Hankie, I think we can wade across."

Wade across? Bad idea. Number One, the

water was running so fast, he'd probably get swept away. Number Two, he couldn't swim. Number Three...

Huh?

Good grief, he had rolled up his pant legs and was wading out into the swirling water!

I barked. "Hey, come back here!"

He kept going, deeper and deeper. As the water came up over his knees, he looked back and gave me the sweetest little-boy smile...and suddenly I felt this awful sense of dread. I KNEW that I would never...I mean, you hear about these things happening to other people, but you never dream...

You probably think this story is going to come to a bad end. Don't you? Go ahead and admit it. Well, it sure seemed to be heading that way, only I did something that really surprised me.

I sprang into the water and took a bite on his hip pocket and started pulling him backwards. He didn't like that and tried to swat me away. "Hankie, quit! I can make it."

I ignored him, which is something we have to do with little boys. I kept pulling and managed to get him back into the shallows. And, oh, he was mad! He drew back his fist and I got the feeling that he wanted to slug me, but just then, we heard a voice in the distance.

"Alfred? Hank? Where are you?"

Alfred looked at me with big eyes. "It's my dad!"

Right, and the kid had come within an inch of punching me in the nose. I cut loose with a barrage of 911 barks. "Over here!"

Moments later, Loper and Slim rode their horses out of the willows on the other side of the creek. They were wearing rain slickers and their hats were soaked. Man oh man, was I glad to see them!

They dismounted and tied their two catch ropes together, which gave them seventy feet of stout line. (Each was carrying a thirty-five foot nylon rope on his saddle, don't you see). After several tosses, Loper managed to land his loop on our side of the creek. Alfred snugged the loop around his middle and he was ready.

Slim yelled, "Grab aholt of the dog, so we don't have to fish him out too!"

The boy wrapped his arms around me and yelled, "Ready!" We entered the water (yipes, it was cold!) and the current swept Alfred off his feet. Fellers, it was a good thing we were tied to a line. That kid *never* would have made it across on his own power.

Out in the middle of the flood, he gave me a grin "You bit me on the hiney."

Exactly right, and the next time he tried to do something crazy, I would do it again.

We made it to the other side, cold and soaked but otherwise okay. Alfred climbed on the horse behind his dad, and with me out front in the Escort position, we headed back to the headquarters—the Return of the Famous Explorers.

Sally May rushed out of the house and scooped up young Daniel Boom in a hug. Everyone was laughing and happy...for a while. But then, well, the hammer came down on young Daniel Boom, as the adults took turns giving him a lecture about naughty little boys who slip out of their rooms and sneak down to the creek.

Sally May said, "Sweetie, why did you go down to the creek? You know we don't allow that. Why, you could have drowned!"

The boy tried to explain. We were playing Wagons West close to the house, but then...well, the horse ran away with the wagon and things got out of hand.

Oops. Her razor eyes shifted to me. "Hank ran off with the wagon and took you all the way down to the creek?"

"Yes, but Mom, listen. Pete made him do it!"

"My cat?"

"Honest. Pete started a fight and Hankie chased him."

My goodness. The silence was amazing. A bolt of truth had just come crashing down from the sky. She glanced toward the iris patch. The villain had vanished, of course, so she turned her gaze on Loper.

He shrugged and said, "Cats."

Then, in a burst of excited words, Alfred told them the rest of the story. Our wagon got hung up in the brush, the storm hit, and we took cover in Madame Moonshine's cave. She held us prisoner then let us go, the creek was flooding and Alfred tried to wade across, only...well, a certain hero pulled him back to shore.

He finished up with, "And Mom, it was the same owl we had in the box this morning. Hankie wasn't going to eat the owl. He saved it from your cat."

Poor Sally May didn't know what to believe, with all the talk about owls and caves and runaway wagons, not to mention the fact that her precious kitty had fallen under a cloud of suspicion. It kind of threw her for a loop. Me? I loved it.

She knelt down in front of the lad, held him by

both shoulders, and looked him straight in the eyes. "Alfred Leroy, we might never find out what really happened, but it doesn't change the rules. 'Children, obey your parents.'"

"Yes ma'am."

"Always obey your parents."

"Yes ma'am."

Her eyes slid around to me. I wilted. "And YOU...if you contributed anything to keeping my child safe from harm..." She searched for words. "...I'm very grateful. Thank you."

Did you hear that? What a finish! All that remained was for us to hug and make up for all the years of Broom Events and misunderstandings. I leaped into her arms and...

Okay, I should have waited for a better time. I mean, dogs who swim rivers aren't always aware of their "wet dog smell," but Sally May sure was. Wow. She gagged and pushed me away, but you know what? Things had turned out pretty well.

Sally May and I had made some progress in patching up our relationship, the boy was safe, we'd gotten a good rain, the cat had been exposed as a villain, and Drover would spend a whole hour with his nose in the corner, repeating, "George ate three blind mice at Grandma's house yesterday."

This case is...

Wait a second. You're probably wondering about Madame Moonshine's "magic word." Was it really magic? Well, I used it and we got help. One way or another, it worked, and on this outfit, that's pretty close to a happy ending.

This case is closed.

Have you read all of Hank's adventures?

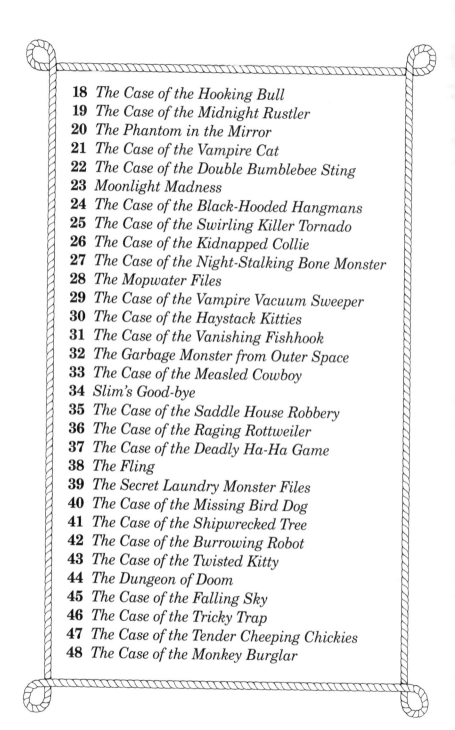

Join Hank the Cowdog's Security Force

Are you a big Hank the Cowdog fan? Then you'll want to join Hank's Security Force! Here is some of the neat stuff you will receive:

Welcome Package
- A Hank paperback
- An Original (19"x25") Hank Poster
- A Hank bookmark

Eight digital issues of
***The Hank Times* with**
- Lots of great games and puzzles
- Stories about Hank and his friends
- Special previews of future books
- Fun contests

More Security Force Benefits
- Special discounts on Hank books, audios, and more
- Special Members-Only section on website

Total value of the Welcome Package and *The Hank Times* is $23.99. However, your two-year membership is **only $7.99** plus $5.00 for shipping and handling.

The following activity is a sample from *The Hank Times*, the official newspaper of Hank's Security Force. Please do not write on this page unless this is your book. Even then, why not just find a scrap of paper?

"Photogenic" Memory Quiz

We all know that Hank has a "photogenic" memory—being aware of your surroundings is an important quality for a Head of Ranch Security. Now you can test your powers of observation.

How good is your memory? Look at the illustration on page 55 and try to remember as many things about it as possible. Then turn back to this page and see how many questions you can answer.

1. How many pockets are on Slim's shirt? 0, 1, or 2?

2. Which of Slim's hands was higher? HIS Left or Right?

3. Was Hank looking Up, Down, or Straight Ahead?

4. Were there any clouds in the sky?

5. Was Slim's belt buckle shape Rectangular, Oval, or "What belt"?

6. How many of Hank's feet were on the ground? 2, 3, 4, or all 5?

Have you visited Hank's official website yet?

www.hankthecowdog.com

Don't miss out on exciting *Hank the Cowdog* games and activities, as well as up-to-date news about upcoming books in the series!

When you visit, you'll find:

- Hank's BLOG, which is updated regularly and is always the first place we announce upcoming books and new products!
- Hank's Official Shop, with tons of great Hank the Cowdog books, audiobooks, games, t-shirts, stuffed animals, mugs, bags, and more!
- Links to Hank's social media, whereby Hank sends out his "Cowdog Wisdom" to fans
- A FREE, printable Map of Hank's Ranch!
- Hank's Music Page where you can listen to songs and even download FREE ringtones!
- A way to sign up for Hank's free email updates
- Sally May's Ranch Round-up Recipes!
- Printable & Colorable Greeting Cards for Holidays

- Articles about Hank and author, John R. Erickson in the news

...AND MUCH, MUCH MORE!

BOOKS
The Collection

FAN ZONE
Fun & Games

AUTHOR
Meet the Creator

STORE
Books & More

search the website   GO

HANK
THE COWDOG

ANNOUNCING:
A sneak peek
at Hank #66

Ever thought of having a
Hank the Cowdog Themed Party?

Hank Plays Cupid:

Find Toys, Games, Books & More at the Hank shop.

GAMES
COME PLAY WITH
HANK & PALS

BOOKS
BROWSE THE ENTIRE
HANK CATALOG

FRIENDS
GET TO KNOW THE
RANCH GANG

Visit Hank's
Facebook
page

Follow Hank
on Twitter

Watch Hank
on YouTube

Follow Hank
on Pinterest

Send Hank
an Email

FROM THE BLOG

JAN 26 Hank is Cupid in Disguise...

JAN 18 The Valentine's Day Robbery! - a Snippet from the Story

DEC 04 Getting SIGNED Hank the Cowdog books for Christmas!

OCT 14 Education Association's lists of recommended books?

VISIT THE BLOG

Hank's Survey
We'd love to know what you think!   GO

Hank's Music.
Free ringtones,
music and more!

MORE

Official Shop
Find books, audio,
toys and more!

LET'S GO

TEACHER'S CORNER
Download fun activity guides,
discussion questions and more.

SALLY MAY'S RECIPES

Discover delicious recipes from
Sally May herself.   GO

Join Hank's Security Force
Get the activity letter and
other cool stuff.

JOIN   SECURITY FORCE

Get the Latest

Keep up with Hank's news
and promotions by signing
up for our e-news.

Looking for The Hank Times
fan club newsletter?

Enter your email address

SIGN UP

Hank in the News

Find out what the media
is saying about Hank.

GO

FEATURED BOOK

The Christmas Turkey Disaster

Now Available!

Hank is in real trouble this time. L....

BUY   READ   LISTEN

HANK

BOOKS
Browse Titles
Buy Books
Audio Samples
Other Books

FAN ZONE
Games
Hank & Friends
Security Force
Educational Stuff

AUTHOR
John Erickson's Bio
Hank in the News
In Concert
Contact John

SHOP
The Books
Store
Get Help
Retailer Info

And, be sure to check out the
Audiobooks!

If you've never heard a *Hank the Cowdog* audiobook, you're missing out on a lot of fun! Each Hank book has also been recorded as an unabridged audiobook for the whole family to enjoy!

Praise for the Hank Audiobooks:

"It's about time the Lone Star State stopped hogging Hank the Cowdog, the hilarious adventure series about a crime solving ranch dog. Ostensibly for children, the audio renditions by author John R. Erickson are sure to build a cult following among adults as well." — *Parade Magazine*

"Full of regional humor . . . vocals are suitably poignant and ridiculous. A wonderful yarn." — *Booklist*

"For the detectin' and protectin' exploits of the canine Mike Hammer, hang Hank's name right up there with those of other anthropomorphic greats...But there's no sentimentality in Hank: he's just plain more rip-roaring fun than the others. Hank's misadventures as head of ranch security on a spread somewhere in the Texas Panhandle are marvelous situation comedy." — *School Library Journal*

"Knee-slapping funny and gets kids reading."

— *Fort Worth Star Telegram*

Love Hank's Hilarious Songs?

Hank the Cowdog's "Greatest Hits" albums bring together the music from the unabridged audiobooks you know and love! These wonderful collections of hilarious (and sometimes touching) songs are unmatched. Where else can you learn about coyote philosophy, buzzard lore, why your dog is protecting an old corncob, how bugs compare to hot dog buns, and much more!

And, be sure to visit Hank's "Music Page" on the official website to listen to some of the songs and download FREE Hank the Cowdog ringtones!

"Audio-Only"
Stories

Ever wondered what those "Audio-Only" Stories in Hank's Official Store are all about? The Audio-Only Stories are *Hank the Cowdog* adventures that have never been released as books. They are about half the length of a typical *Hank* book, and there are currently seven of them. They have run as serial stories in newspapers for years and are now available as audiobooks!

Teacher's Corner

Know a teacher who uses Hank in their classroom? You'll want to be sure they know about Hank's "Teacher's Corner"! Just click on the link on the homepage, and you'll find free teachers' aids, such as a printable map of Hank's ranch, a reading log, coloring pages, blog posts specifically for teachers and librarians, and much more!

John R. Erickson, a former cowboy, has written numerous books for both children and adults and is best known for his acclaimed *Hank the Cowdog* series. The H*ank* series began as a self-publishing venture in Erickson's garage in 1982 and has endured to become one of the nation's most popular series for children and families. Through the eyes of Hank the Cowdog, a smelly, smart-aleck Head of Ranch Security, Erickson gives readers a glimpse into daily life on a cattle ranch in the West Texas Panhandle. His stories have won a number of awards, including the Audie, Oppenheimer, Wrangler, and Lamplighter Awards, and have been translated into Spanish, Danish, Farsi, and Chinese. USA Today calls the *Hank the Cowdog* books "the best family entertainment in years." Erickson lives and works on his ranch in Perryton, Texas, with his family.

Gerald L. Holmes is a largely self-taught artist who grew up on a ranch in the Oklahoma Panhandle. He has illustrated the *Hank the Cowdog* books and serial stories, in addition to numerous other cartoons and textbooks, for over thirty years, and his paintings have been featured in various galleries across the United States. He and his wife live in Perryton, Texas, where they raised their family, and where he continues to paint his wonderfully funny and accurate portrayals of modern American ranch life to this day.